ALSO BY NATASHA RADOJČIĆ

Homecoming

YOU

DON'T

HAVE

TO

LIVE

HERE

YOU
DON'T
HAVE
TO
LIVE
HERE

A NOVEL

Natasha Radojčić

RANDOM HOUSE

NEW YORK

Published in the United States by Random
House, an imprint of The Random House
Publishing Group, a division of Random
House, Inc., New York.

RANDOM HOUSE and colophon are registered
trademarks of Random House, Inc.

An earlier version of chapter 3 was published as
"Shades of Mango" in *Tin House,* Winter 2004.

LIBRARY OF CONGRESS CATALOGING-IN-
PUBLICATION DATA
Radojčić, Natasha.
You don't have to live here : a novel / Natasha
Radojčić.
p.   cm.
ISBN 1-4000-6236-5
1. Teenage girls—Fiction.   2. New York (N.Y.)—
Fiction.   3. Immigrants—Fiction.   4. Travelers—
Fiction.   5. Yugoslavia—Fiction.
6. Greece—Fiction.   7. Cuba—Fiction.   I. Title.
PS3618.A355Y68 2005
813'.6—dc22   2004050764

Printed in the United States of America
on acid-free paper

Random House website address:
www.atrandom.com

9 8 7 6 5 4 3 2 1

FIRST EDITION

for Mom, not to worry

ACKNOWLEDGMENTS

Many individuals have contributed their enormous talent and endless patience to this book: Gabrielle Bordwin, Evan Camfield, David Gates, Stephanie Higgs, Matthew Kellogg, Pei Koay, Randee Marullo, Daniel Menaker, Azar Nafisi, Gary Shteyngart, Emilie Stewart. Without their tireless efforts and collaboration, I never would have been able to finish.

Some travel alongside my life requiring only a first name: Angelo, Angie, Bojana, Christine, Chuck, D., Djordje, Em, Giulia, Igor, Janer, JBZ, Matteo, Max, Marcia, Nuna, Olja, Pep, Rachel, Roberto, Sakeena, Sally, Shiggs, Sue, Teča, Tetka, and the Killington crew. You have an extraordinary talent for hope! I love you.

Finally, I wish to thank the many anonymous, faceless, but unforgotten victims of injustices human beings inflict upon each other. Your flourishing despite unspeakable suffering humbles me, inspires me, and gives me the courage and reason to persevere.

1

What remains of the early days begins
with an image of my foot. It's soiled and
swollen from the heat. It presses into the
chair. The chair is ordinary: four legs and
a seat. Part of an average waiting room.
The waiting room is in a Mental Building.
My other foot dangles.

Mother is inside talking with the Specialist and the
Policeman with the most stripes.

A gray-haired woman sits across from me. Her lips are
smacking, mouthing, Help me, help me please, each time her
attendant looks away. The creases on her face are deep and
dirty. Her eyes heave with fear. I wonder where her family is.
Then another attendant arrives, followed by a woman with a
neat bun. They force the gray-haired woman to stand up. She
stumbles a little, her arms caught behind her, and she
whispers to me, Don't leave me, please don't leave me.

I am afraid for her, afraid of where they are taking her. But I don't know how to help. Be careful, I call after her. Keep dry.

I am almost fifteen. I ran away, and the runaway children have to be examined by the Specialist. The Policeman who brought me here asked why I ran. I don't know, I said. I just didn't want to go home. I sat at the train station, under the swinging metal sign that said Track 8, and watched the soldiers walk through the steam with their big bags full of promises to our country, Yugoslavia.

Months before that I didn't exist. Nothing of me existed. Just my long hair, the ribbons I wore in it. Mother picked them out. They were blue and yellow. I stayed in my room reading most of the day. Mother came home at night, lay down in the bedroom we shared, and sighed about the harshness of life, of the smoky heat in the classroom where she taught, of my father's betrayal. Then I fled to the TV.

Our TV is black and white, shameful. We are the poorest part of our family. Poverty doesn't stop Mother. She buys an old piano. For her girl, she says. For her baby girl. The piano is part of the ambition she has for me. I am going to amount to something. Be a lady. I loathe the instrument and I paint it white with cheap wall paint. The thin coat drips in black and gray stripes. It gathers inside the carved crevices and traps an unfortunate fly.

What did you do? Mother asks, pointing at the slow fluttering of the dying wings.

I wanted a white piano.

But look! It's disgusting.

I know, I say.

. . .

I never really understood Mother. Not after many years had passed, her death, my marriage, my divorce. The naïveté with which she pursued life. Her stubborn hunger after my improvement. Maybe it was the extraordinary poverty in which she had grown up that shaped and scarred her. Her grades were average. She had nothing, except for her beauty, that pale and cold perfection. It slayed men. After her divorce they came around and waited for her sign to stay. Any sign would have been sufficient. But she never offered.

. . .

The day before I ran, I beat poor Yana, the ugliest girl in the entire school. The passive way she surrendered to her ungainly body, the dullness in her slaughterhouse eyes, infuriated me. At fourteen she had already capitulated. I beat her with my fists, pulled her hair, and spit on her. The other children circled around me shouting, Crazy, crazy. Mother was summoned. Father as well, but he didn't come. I am the only child whose father never comes. The headmistress insisted that she didn't know why everybody called me crazy, but it was enough that other children, well fathered and well mannered, thought I was. Look, she conspired into Mother's delicately shaped ear, she wrote a story about the Devil and Angels and Wings and Chains and Heaven, and there is no

room for such things in the mind of a true Communist youth.
No room at all. Please get a firm grip. Or else.

Please, I begged Mother after the meeting. I want to be a
writer.

You need to be something distinguished, not loose. A
doctor, a lawyer. A rich wife, she ordered.

Being distinguished was far beyond my reach, but I didn't
want to disappoint her. So I decided to disappear.

I ran.

And slept on the bench. The train-station attendant
noticed me and asked me how old I was. Almost fifteen, I said,
and he disbelieved. You are so broad, so fleshy, so ample, he
said. His breath was moist and close. You must be eighteen.

Fifteen, I said and peered at the grime lodged underneath
his fingernails. It angered him.

The Policeman appeared and asked, Why aren't you in
school, where are your books, your parents, and where on
earth do you live? He grabbed my arm and led me to the car.
We passed the attendant, who yelled,

Eighteen.

. . .

Even then I knew how to rouse them, the men. A little girl. A
lost girl. I can see that image clearly. The young body is bent
slightly forward, looking at the floor. The eyes are humble,
always connected to the ground, while sending something
into the air. It made them come: the attendant, the Policeman. It makes them come still. Rush.

Even then I was better at it than most women. Better even than Mother. I never succumbed to skin creams, clothes, intrigues. I never tried to be exquisite. I never tried. I was just thirsty. The thirst was always there. Long before I stopped the drinking and the heroin, long before I even started it. The thirst attached itself to me, changed me. I became thirst, and the men knew. Even today, right this minute, I am thirsty.

. . .

Brought home in the police car, for the neighbors to see, Shame, shame, Mother cried. Nothing like this has ever happened. Once, a little girl was found wandering around the neighborhood in her underwear. Her family, who were some sort of war refugees, broke into the basement of our building and squatted. Mother came home pale that day. She threatened to kill herself if such shame tainted the underwear of our family. The girl had been tampered with, Uncle said. We are nothing like them, Grandmother comforted. We are not cattle. Lining up during the discount hours at the butcher's on Tuesdays, feeding our children with cheap rice and small pieces of calf's heart and chicken gizzards. We are not. We eat. We eat as much as we want. Big pieces of fresh meat, chunks of smoked cold cuts, pies filled with ground beef and cheese. We earned it. Fought Nazis for it. We are hard and full of pride.

Grandmother bore nine healthy children, six of them boys. She lost her husband in World War II. Her youngest wasn't even kicking in her belly yet, she said. The next two still crawling. She was our pillar before senility turned her back into a child. Now she spends most of her time resting far up in the mountains of western Bosnia, and wears a diaper.

Mother and I live alone. A month after my birth, Mother abandoned her newlywed nest located in an attic of somebody's house, the only thing Father could afford, and returned to Grandmother's apartment. Now we live next door to the working Gypsy colony. The colony is a result of Tito's idea of "Brotherhood and Unity" among the many people in our country, even the darkly colored. Now Gypsies with jobs are allowed to occupy the small cardboard shacks propped up with planks and mud. So long as they are employed as cleaners for a nearby train station they can maintain a solid roof over their heads.

People visit our apartment. We are respectable, worthy of a visit. A knock on the door, *Salaam alikum* if the visitors are Muslim, or just a hello if God doesn't matter. Shoes are left outside. We are Communists, but walking barefoot indoors is an unwritten custom in Muslim homes not even the revolution can break. The coffee is ground, the water boiled, our legs folded under our bodies in the Turkish style.

I am young, so I listen. There are complaints about the godless Gypsy dancing, the dangerous trading in young girls' flesh, and how government and the police turn the other way. There is talk of war. Of heroism and wounds. Uncle pulls up his trousers to show six holes. Three dumdum bullets. I kiss the wounds. It's my duty.

. . .

The Specialist's waiting room walls are covered with strange pictures of children and their parents. They are doing everyday things, walking, talking. The smiles on their faces are extraordinary. I wonder why they smile so much. The Socialist Mental Building is new, but the politicians always steal the concrete and sand for their mistresses and families. The floor is already slanted and the secretary's chair keeps sliding.

The Specialist looks credible in an expensive blue suit. He asks to speak to Mother first. I am anxious to hear what he has to say about my ailments. Everybody has a theory, but I expect his to be the most accurate. I imagine a series of diagnoses. I eat too much, sleep too little. I am not a diligent student. I pass out on the neighbors' floor so as not to have to return home. Mother's eldest sister, Aunt Dika, says, The little fox woke up, looked down between her legs, and realized she had a slit in need of filling. So she forgot herself. Marry her off.

Mother floats out elegant and remote as always. My beautiful Momma who I always want to kiss. She carries the same look on her face she gives anyone who's beneath her: our butcher, the cleaning lady, her many gentleman callers. The Specialist follows. He droops his face like a good boy caught the first time he'd attempted anything bad. The money spent on the suit was a waste. Whatever his ideas were, they had been rejected. Mother halts in front of me.

You and I are leaving, she says. Uncle is coming to dinner.

. . .

Uncle is an engineer. Best in his class. Mother is a professor. They are both fair and each other's favorite. I am like my dark part-Gypsy father who I am never allowed to mention. Uncle has brought along his first son. Cousin has blue eyes and blond hair. Everything he does is perfect. Mother admires his athleticism, the symmetry of his muscles. Calls him Son. He wiggles his fingers between my legs while Uncle compliments Mother's cooking.

. . .

It's dark. A faraway police siren travels through the window and I am afraid it will wake Cousin, who is finally asleep. Mother said, Cousin should stay in your room again, even if he sleeps on the floor. He is such a good influence. Mother and her favorite brother are happy their children get along so well. I am afraid he'll climb up on top of me and hurt me between my legs like he always does when we share a room, and I don't sleep. When he rolls over and it looks like he is about to wake up, I pretend I have to go to the bathroom and I stay there as long as I can.

My drawings are sprawled across the floor. I wish there was something sharper than a pencil to hurt him with. He snores lightly. His fair curls hang over his pretty face like new leaves. He is almost as pretty as Mother. That gets him out of trouble. I wish he wasn't family. I wish a lovely boy like him, everybody's favorite, would be interested in me for real, not just at night. Then I could brag that he loves me. Then I could like the things he does to me.

I want to count my money. I have been saving for two

years now. But I am afraid he'll wake up and steal it. Morning is dawning and the trains are clattering in, bringing cleaning women, bread, meat, milk, and cheese fresh for the market, baskets full of potatoes. I hope our breakfast will be rich, eggs and bacon. We all eat bacon. Even Grandmother. We lied to her and said it was just fried chicken skin, and she devoured it, saying it was the best fried chicken skin she'd ever had. We knew she'd turned slow and believed us; but we also knew whoever tricks a Muslim, good or ex, into eating the dirty *domuz* is going to hell on the Last Day, when Allah brings forth the resurrection of all the dead, and pronounces the judgment of every person in accordance with his deeds.

2

I thought Mother would beat me for
running. She had hit me before, with a
belt a few times, but mostly she chased
me around the dining room table with a
slipper or a clog. Once she hit me harder
than she thought I deserved. Then she
came to my bedroom at night and brushed
and braided my hair, something she
hadn't done in years.

This time, nothing. A quiet glance at me and then away,
then she collected her pillows, the little things she kept by
her bed—Grandfather's stout black-and-white army picture,
a bottle of some French ladies' cognac covered with candle
wax drippings, a bronze statue of a hen hovering over a nest of
eggs, the warm-weather cover, the light blanket—and moved
silently to the living room.

I sat on the bed and stayed like that all night. In the
morning she knocked at my door twice. That became our new

signal—time for you to come out of there and join the normal people.

It's Sunday. I cut my ballet lessons. My teacher, ninety-year-old Russian ballerina Madame Voronec, is blind. The entire class sneaks out right after the secretary takes attendance. Demi, demi, grand, grand, she commands the empty room. The accompanist, Mr. Korishnik, stays there and practices jazz on the piano, which is of excellent quality. He likes the secretary. Her legs are long and she sits like a lady.

I run to the black market and exchange my deutschmarks for dollars. It's easy. Nobody around here wants dollars. After today's 30 I have 965 total. Nobody knows this yet, but I am moving to America.

The Gypsy lady at the far end of the market and I have been doing business together for a while. She always looks at my dark skin and my clean clothes suspiciously. The two are a mismatch.

Her green-and-red-fringed scarf mingles in the crowd on the other side of the market. Her goods are laid out on the hood of an old Volkswagen. I wonder who in the world buys silly knickknacks like that—unwrapped candy stuck together, crooked rolls of Scotch tape, strange pens—but her pheasants and rabbits are fresh and young.

She is also selling a clock.

A true beauty. She flaunts its Venetian glass and good mahogany. Cheap.

Two brass angels with hand-engraved wings rock back and forth in the rhythm of the time passing. Mother would love it. Her eyes glisten at pretty things.

How much? I ask.

Fifty.

Robbing people today, aren't you?

Fifty, she repeats.

No way.

It's an original. Belonged to a countess. She and I were friends, back in the glory days of countesses. She gave it to me before she ran far across the river.

I just want to change to dollars.

Are you one of us? she asks me as she takes the money.

I don't answer.

You're dark, she says.

So?

Did you steal these deutschmarks? she asks.

Did you steal the clock?

It really did belong to a countess.

I'm sure, I say.

As sure as you don't have a drop of Gypsy blood in your veins?

Father is part Gypsy, part Austrian, part Serb. I inherited his black eyes, chocolate hair, skin that browns in the sun, and love for languages and harmonious shapes. The aunts say I inherited his mouth as well; all golden and full of promise, with no delivery.

I guess Father would have made a decent parent had he not been infected with the disease of bad choices and weak character. By the time he met Mother, he had been married several times. After Mother left, he married one more time, fathered one more child, and eventually settled for bachelorhood, which he was best suited for.

Father's father was a red-haired half-Gypsy. He was also

a famously violent man, known for bursting through closed gates with a three-horse-driven carriage after midnight. The rumors say Grandfather killed many men and buried them inside the well on his land. Years later a barrel of powder mysteriously exploded inside the well, shattering all the evidence.

Grandfather left home at seven when his Gypsy mother married a sixty-year-old man. The new husband put a blade to Grandfather's throat the day after the wedding and said, I am the master now. Grandfather packed a pound of cheese, a pound of bread, and a dry leg of lamb into a saddlebag he stole from his new father, and walked two hundred miles across the frozen steppe until he reached the cavalry camp and got himself a job as a groom.

Father's mother, Marta, was a pious girl, an only child of a rich Austrian settler, born deep in a December night right before Christmas cursed with a clubfoot. She never exhibited any signs of passion or madness until one day, hobbling back from the church dragging her bad leg through the mud, she saw a young dark thing covered with strange orange hair breaking a mare. The obedient way the mare bent her young mane down to my grandfather's ginger-haired arm before she was even harnessed unsettled Grandmother and she drew close. She instantly fell in love with the acrid smell of his manly torso, with the submissiveness of the freshly broken mare, and would not hear of any other suitor. They were married soon after. Grandfather ended up a rich man.

. . .

My parents' marriage was as unlikely as it was short. They had little or nothing in common other than the wrong idea of each other. At the time of their meeting, smooth, irresistible Father was studying classics after a brief attempt at medicine and law. He was also having a childless affair with the dumpy, nearsighted female colleague who typed his articles. Meanwhile, Mother was furious at her soon-to-be ex-fiancé for bestowing expensive jewelry on some shady folksinger with big breasts and no talent.

My parents' romance was a typical melodramatic Eastern European liaison, with insane intensity enough to temporarily erase all the memories of their humble Balkan-peasant beginnings and the harshness that comes with them. Mother was dazzled by Father's stories of the intricate Paris rococo architecture he had never visited but talked of with authority, and of the complicated relationships among the flawed anthropomorphic gods of Olympus.

. . .

Years later, Mother was dead already, and I was walking with Father through a red-light district in Istanbul. From the window of a gloriously obvious bordello, framed by heavy crimson curtains and moody light, four prostitutes recognized him and called out his name. Bora, *salaam.* They were excited to see him. He stopped and waved back. All four ran downstairs and onto the street to meet us. One of them smirked and whispered something into his ear. Father hugged me and proudly said, My daughter, Alexandra, Sasha. Pretty, pretty, she said and kissed my cheek.

It wasn't the seductive stories about Zeus and Poseidon's struggle over the throne, how lovely and bright Apollo was, how gentle and delicate the faithful Orpheus, that captured Mother's heart. It was the open invitation and passion Father had in his initial approach to everyone he met that made Mother feel like a queen.

Mother's icy, measured beauty was no match for Father's lies. The pedestal to which her looks elevated her above the rest of us rendered her inexperienced and innocent. She believed that the apartment was Father's, only a puny fragment of his handsome inheritance; that the crippled woman sitting silently by the window was just his aunt, who would be returning to her family next month. Better for her really, he said, for they were even wealthier.

Pregnant four months after they met and a month after they were married, Mother continued believing Father's myths for another seven months, until a man in a gray coat came, told her he was the landlord and that the nonpaying bastard, his retarded mother, and whoever you are, missy, a dummy for sure, who else gets in a baby way with a charlatan, were about to be evicted. And then the truth struck: All pretty words and no pennies. Mother cried into her mother-in-law's there-there-pretty-girl lap. The two had become friends. When she was done crying, she packed the five cloth diapers she had, what would become my favorite blanket, a few trinkets she had received as wedding presents. And she left. I was born thirty-two days after. And twenty-seven days after my first birthday Mother and Father were legally divorced.

3

The parched Eastern European summer of '81 dries up the riverbanks, which hum with the buzz of newborn mosquitoes, and the shriveling crops warn of the barren harvest, but Mother and I are saved from scarcity. Her most distinguished brother, the firstborn, Malik, has been appointed ambassador to Cuba and he has bought our plane tickets.

Malik is a real success, the pride of our family. Tito, the president of our righteous and brave country, appointed him to this position himself, and honored him with a gold pin. Fidel Castro complimented the proficiency of his Spanish, and his picture appeared in an important Cuban newspaper.

Take the bad girl with you, the Aunts advise. Being under the same roof with a serious, respectable man will be constructive. I am packed in one suitcase, filled with homely and humble outfits designed to steer me in the right direction.

I miss the European drought. Breathing in Cuba feels like inhaling water. We arrive and the shirts stick to our bodies that seem too tall and too white among the short brown people who greet us on the tarmac. Uncle fits among them like Gulliver. He seems happy to see Mother, even happier to see the pretty, pale all-girl choir here to represent Yugoslavia at the International Youth Festival. Uncle loves pretty women, and marvels at the way their elongated limbs fuss about in the heavy sun.

Let me help you with your suitcase, he tells one of them. The one Mother pointed out as vulgar during the flight. The driver takes our baggage.

. . .

There are no seasons here. No such change around the girth of the planet; just the exhausting morning heat, then rainy afternoons, followed by the evening heat. The perpetual water flow has transformed my skin and my hair. Both grow thicker, heavier. I cut my T-shirts, shorten a pair of pants way above my knees. The frumpy skirts are still inside the suitcase.

I spend the first few boring mornings playing soccer against the cook's assistant. A grown man of maybe forty, he lets me dribble the deflated ball between his legs and beat him. A swift career move, as he has his eye on the soon-to-retire driver's position. Getting on the ambassador's good side is a wise choice. Those who drive have access to gas coupons. Just like at home, gas is everything in Cuba.

After a month I am slowly settled. The kitchen is my haven. I love the clank of the dishes, the hissing of the pans, the piercing chatter of the house parrots. The way they fret each time the sizzling oven door opens and the scorching steam surges through their cages.

Lupe, the main cook, serves me cheese sandwiches. Makes the gardener laugh. I don't know his name. He is chocolate-dark and he never sits down while I am around and never looks at me directly.

Mother stays away from the kitchen, says the jungle heat makes her want to eat more, which is bad for the waist. Aunt Ludmila thinks it's bad to spend time with the help. It's common, she says. She has blossomed since we arrived here. Our Muslim names mark no shame at all; the color of the skin bares the distinction in this land. We are the whites, better than everybody. Here Aunt Ludmila's paleness is priceless.

At home, the feeble pasty color of her skin was often blamed for Cousin Juma's mental condition. Juma was born with a gaping hole in her stomach, a belly open to the world. Aunt Ludmila claimed her to be a miracle, a precious miracle destined to be cherished. She was kept concealed from the world. In the darkness of her room, she read the *Encyclopaedia Britannica* and memorized every detail about the beautiful actresses. When she was allowed at the family dinner table, she spun intricate stories. Her favorite was Harlean Carpenter, born March 3, 1911, in Kansas City, which was not in Kansas at all. Juma told us that young Harlean, believing she was soon to be a huge star, adopted her mother's maiden name and rebaptized herself as Jean Harlow. Then in 1932 her husband, Paul Bern's, unfortunate death shook Hollywood. There were rumors of suicide. Of secret liaisons. Of a young lover. Jean Harlow was 5 feet 3 inches, 36-26-36,

108 pounds, Juma said. None of us had a clue what a foot, an inch, or a pound meant. I imagined they were something wonderful, if they inaugurated the lovely Ms. Harlow into the company of Ava, the raven-haired, green-eyed vixen who married Frank Sinatra; Rita Hayworth, who, Juma taught us, was actually Mexican; and of course the French sex-kitten petite Brigitte, who loved animals as much as she loved cutting her wrists with razors.

. . .

I hardly ever see Uncle. He is always at the port. The ships under the Yugoslavian flag carry special cargo from Russia, things that keep the Communism in the Caribbean afloat, he says. It's an honor.

During the afternoon downpours I swim in the oval-shaped pool. When it starts to thunder Mother orders me inside. She is afraid of lightning. Afraid of my getting electrocuted. It had happened to me once already; a toaster rattled my teeth. Mother says the lightning is like millions of toasters. I try to ignore her, but when the thudding sky is too loud for her, the pool gate turns up locked. Then I kill my time wandering about the enormous hallways of our splendid two-story mansion, with an octagonal ballroom and endless staircases. The original family must have been prosperous. Pious too, since they built the house so close to the church. I can see the sharp steeple from my window. The sugar fields are on the other side. They are monitored by the army.

I seek clues, traces. Who was the husband? I wonder. Was the wife gentle and sweet? What color were the children? Did they learn to walk early? Or were they brawny like me, and walked late, when the poor legs were strong enough to carry all that body, as Mother anguished? What were the secrets the musty tropical concrete witnessed? Liaisons? Treasures? I find nothing.

There is a door in the ceiling in the middle of the kitchen. I ask Lupe what's up there. She points her pretty brown eyes sharply at me and says harshly, *Nada*. Then she returns to ripping the feathers off the dead chicken that had soaked in the boiling water. She tugs on the bird severely, and its broken neck dangles off the kitchen table. I am surprised. Several days before, I watched Lupe tenderly hand-feed Kotorita, the parrot, struck down by a bird disease. She used a cotton towel to clean her beak, eyes, and feet. Lupe is even nice to Juma. She smears the yellow ham fat over toast when Aunt Ludmila isn't watching. It's Juma's favorite food, and she calls Lupe Lupita, which means little and sweet.

I sneak the ladder from the broom closet during the afternoon siesta. Uncle is snoring in the shade of the cabana. The Cuban rum inebriates him much faster than Bosnian plum brandy. The thumping showers outside the window muffle the screeching of the attic cover as I lift it up. At first I see nothing. A bleached plywood storage room with bags of flour, beans, and rice and bottles of oil. The dried meats Mother and I smuggled across the border hang against the wall. We brought five sheep legs. One has already been served. There are only three hanging. Most Cubans can't buy meat and I understand why they would steal.

There are two small windows. The raindrops bounce off the beefy leaves, barely moving them. Some sort of a jungle bird squawks and flutters away through the downpour. From the window in my bedroom at home I could see a single poplar, stripped of its greenness by the freezing eastern wind. And far beyond the poplar, the sooty Danube coiling behind the dirty cargo trains lugging coal from Hungary.

There is a big stain on the windowpane. Without getting closer I recognize blood. I once saw a freshly beheaded rabbit stain a windowpane. My screaming grandmother, the executioner, blamed the blunt knife for not slicing the artery right. The drops of color on this windowpane are the same. Somehow I know they didn't sprinkle from a rabbit's throat.

I climb down quietly and run into Lupe's concerned face. She knows to whom the drops belonged. *No se preocupe,* I say and offer her my hand. *Silencio.*

Before dinner I carefully examine the walls in the den. The Communists destroyed all the portraits. Several new coats of paint haven't covered the dents where they hung for generations. After we sit down to eat, under the chandelier bigger than my childhood bed, I ask Uncle who lived in the house before the Revolution. The damn capitalist bourgeois, he grunts. The exploiters. Those who took more than they needed from the poor, much more than they needed. How are we different, I wonder, but have the good sense not to ask.

. . .

My going to school is postponed. I am relieved. I can't understand a word, and even the tallest boys are shorter than me. I'll be starting the English school next month, Mother warns, which means harder math, law, and physics. She's made grand plans for my future. Cuba is a great opportunity, she says. It will open many, many doors for me.

The embassy is giving a huge banquet and even Fidel is expected to attend. Our house is in an uproar for three days with preparations. Special soldiers armed with heavy machine guns snoop all over the house. One of them tries to get a better look while I am swimming. Our cocker spaniel barks him away. The dog hates uniforms.

Aunt Ludmila's been hard after Lupe and the extra help employed to assist with the banquet. She clutches at her reddening throat, a thing she does when she is nervous, and she screams after she tastes a sauce Lupe made.

Disaster, disaster, she cries. You can't expect a girl, a Cuban girl, to understand complex European dishes.

Sorry, *Señora*. Lupe looks at the floor embarrassed. I am angry. I want to grab Aunt Ludmila by her badly dyed hair. I want to yank hard and scream back, European? You grew up barefoot, chasing runaway cows and sucking bee-sting venom out of your calloused feet. Leave Lupe alone. But I am too much of a coward and resign myself to offering Lupe a consoling look.

A young boy signed up to bring in the baskets of veg-etables and wine gapes before the colossal Viennese cake. He's never seen such a thing, he says. Cubans get coupons for flour in the *liberta*, ration book. The cake had devoured fifty eggs, three pounds of sugar, and three pounds of butter. There is very little flour left in the bag apportioned to an average Cuban family for a month's supply.

Get out of here, little idiot, Aunt Ludmila bellows.

I catch Lupe's glance. Ludmila may be dim and slow at

times, but she is usually not cruel. At least never in front of strangers. She must be worried that Cousin Juma might find a way to escape the woman hired to keep her in her bedroom, a nurse of some sort, and start on the famous actresses and embarrass our country. Or that Fidel Castro, a reputed admirer of redheads, might fall for Mother, who by far outshines the legendary Hollywood beauties, and create an international scandal. From Juma I learned that the mighty Rita Hayworth was really short and drank too much. Mother is tall and I have never seen her drunk.

For days, dressmakers discreetly visited her room, measured her delicate waste, her regal shoulders, her perfect legs. With sharp needles, their fine hands shaped the fabric to fit Mother's beauty. The help is so wonderfully cheap and accurate around here, Mother says. She is a daughter of an illiterate woman, born in a house without indoor plumbing, and yet she bears her newfound distinction with the ease one might attribute to generations of careful breeding.

The outcome is exceptional. Mother is ravishing. I want to kiss her like the men have kissed her before and forget how ugly I am. She shimmers in a green gown, her light-burgundy tresses held up with the diamond pin we, the compassionate and just visitors from a Communist sister-country, recently purchased with illegal Western European currency from the impoverished Cubans on the street.

. . .

Benya the driver is assigned the task of driving me to the ice-cream parlor and a movie during the first hours of the banquet, until my bedtime. Mother wants Juma to go with us. She says it would do her good to be independent, get out of the house, even if the nurse comes along. Then there is some commotion upstairs. Juma, who's been agitated since the morning, is in the hallway naked. The soldiers are peeking from under their humbly bowed heads, suppressing laughs. The nurse is complaining in a fast-paced Spanish. *Maldita sea, arruinar!* Ruined. Her only sweater has been bitten through and she's had enough.

Together, Mother and Aunt Ludmila regain control over the unfortunate family heritage. The crazy girl is briskly wrapped in a tablecloth. Mother brings her best brush and offers to untangle Juma's hair. As does everybody else, Juma melts before Mother and concedes. The ebony handle glides slowly up and down as Aunt Ludmila offers her daughter some sweet lemonade. Juma refuses, but changes her mind after Mother tells her fresh lemon is good for acne. I wonder what kind of lemonade makes an agitated person so sleepy so quickly. As Juma's eyes close, Mother puts the brush down and looks at Ludmila the same way Lupe and I sometimes do.

I follow Benya, who is telling something very strict to the soldiers, down the stairs to our Ford LTD, the only American car I have ever been inside. I love the car and I have washed it twice. I am glad Juma is not coming. I'd rather eat my ice cream and watch my movie in peace.

. . .

The streets are brimming. Benya drives slowly toward old Havana, cursing *maricón* and *coño* at the traffic. The International Youth Festival is at its peak. Everyone is outside. On the corner of Obrapia and Aguiar I see some of the Yugoslavian choir members.

Let's stop, *por favor*? I ask Benya.

He looks at me, then at the girls, and I whisper, I won't tell, won't tell. I didn't about the blood on the attic window, either. He looks at me again and I see he knows what happened to the people, and that maybe he too thinks it wasn't right.

Okay.

The girls are gathered around a Cuban band. The drummer has only one arm and is beating the other conga with his foot. There are three guitar players. The girls are wearing their stage clothes—long, plain black velvet skirts, starched white shirts. They are singing *Guantanamera, guajira guantanamera*. The sweating air juices up the fabric, and the clothes don't look so plain anymore.

The girl Mother pointed out as cheap, the one whose suitcase Uncle offered to carry, the pretty Gordana, is spinning around while the men are clapping. She has taken her bra off. I can see her nipples through her shirt, darker and bigger than Mother's exquisite pink dots. The men around her get louder each time she lifts her arms up and they can get a better look. *Ochun Kole-Kole, Ochun Kole-Kole*, they chant to the wicked sorceress, the lady of the river, the goddess. I think maybe it's not so bad to have big, dark nipples like Father's Gypsy grandmother, or these coffee-colored people, and I promise to try not to curse the two brown spots I see growing in the mirror.

A young man snakes slowly out of the crowd toward Gordana. He is darker than the rest. Black like charcoal and shirtless. He grabs her by her hand and starts swirling her around like I have never seen before. The Cubans are clapping even harder, and the drummer is beating faster and shaking his half-arm, and sweat clamps Gordana's shirt to her nipples, and the crowd is now screaming *Kole-Kole, Kole-Kole,* moving their hips, until Benya touches my shoulder and says, *Vámonos.*

No, no, por favor, let me look, let me look please. He smiles and whispers, I'll go get the ice cream, so we have something to take home.

Gracias.

I am alone in the crowd. No one is watching me. I shake too. Scared at first; scared that Mother will come looking, making sure I eat the right kind of ice cream, and that there are no dangerous toasters or lightning in Old Havana. Then I am no longer afraid, and I start to shake, to bend, to quiver, and an older bronze-colored man comes near me, leans over, *Un poquito blanquita.* He rubs his dirty hand up toward my shoulder.

What are you? he asks.

Gitana, I say.

He throws his head back, flashing his blackened gums. His fedora falls on the ground. I knew it, he says, I knew it. One of us.

. . .

The night is longer, even hotter, than the afternoon. The endless Cuban summer night, tossing, sweating, rolling, thinking about Gordana's dancing partner's chest. The music

accompanying the banquet downstairs is stifling. I am
ashamed of myself, ashamed of my shaking. I want ice cream.
I want my bad mouth full of cold ice cream. I would bite into it
and press my teeth into it until it throbs and erases the afternoon, the blackened gums, *Gitana, Gitana, Kole-Kole,* and the
sweat.

Benya left a paper box filled with vanilla in the freezer. I
refused it when he offered on the drive back. Didn't want to
be a child. I do now. I want to feel like a little girl again, want
my ice cream. There is a strange change in me, and while I
tiptoe downstairs toward the kitchen, past the armed soldier
falling asleep with his head propped up against his machine
gun, past the servants wearing tuxedos, I no longer want to
bend my head down and look away like I used to.

I peek inside the ballroom. The dresses and suits whiz by
me, methodically, deliberately. The rhythms claim conquest.
People of this room have won. Crystal glasses glitter over the
coy smiles of the expensive ladies, and assured gentlemen
mix their important stories into the sweltering mustiness.

Mother is the star. She is dancing with Fidel, whose green
uniform is flat and not at all luscious compared to her dress.
I am proud she outshines him. Hand grenades and a pistol
hang around his waist. I change my mind about him falling
for Mother. It's not that I'm afraid. No—I grew up around
weapons, blasted the head off my first duck at seven. No, this
is not fear. The armed bearded man whose hands are on
Mother's body had something to do with the stain in the attic.
I am sure. I don't want him touching her.

The kitchen is empty. I sit behind the door and feel tears, a
terrible hot bubbling of tears. Something is irrevocably lost.

Lupe passes me, without noticing. I can see how uncomfortable she is in the stiff gray dress Aunt Ludmila made her wear for Fidel. Then she sees me and gently whispers, What is the matter, child, don't cry here. Her hands, tired from chopping, pulling, cleaning, all day long, offer a hug. I obey like a little girl. I can still be kind to Lupe. But her hug is no longer enough.

. . .

I ride my bike and listen to the Youth Choir practice every day. I wear makeup. Mother is happy I wear makeup, says she was worried I'd stay a boy forever. Aunt Ludmila disapproves, says it's too early. If she is allowed to paint herself now, what will ensue at seventeen, eighteen? Ensue? This big word provokes me. I steal her lipstick in retaliation. She wears red and it's the color I want. I put it on once I'm outside, using the bike mirror. My lips are red, and the older Cuban ladies say *puta* when I go by them. Their husbands, I think, don't mind as much.

The beggar ladies smile at me. *Qué bonita*, one of them calls me. I come back the next day and sit with her. *Qué bonita*, she calls me again, and strokes my hair with her fingers, her nails cracked from sleeping on the street concrete. The next day I find her passed out. I take my lipstick and put the red on her mouth. She wakes up startled and grabs my arm like a drunk man would, but then she recognizes me, *Bonita*, and smiles and falls back to sleep with red *puta* lips smiling.

I sit in the back of the concert hall and watch the choir girls. They are tired. The conductor has heard that Brezhnev, the Russian president, might show up for the final performance. The posters of him shaking hands with Fidel hang over the entire lengths of Havana's skyscrapers. If Brezhnev liked the girls, it could mean a good chance for the conductor at the musical academy in Moscow. The conductor is also a championship swimmer, a sharpshooting winner, and a legend in long-distance running. He will not stop. The girls are complaining they'll have no throats left to make a peep if the bushy-eyebrowed Russian does show up. Finally they are dismissed. Gordana's dark-skinned dance partner helps her off the stage.

Like me, he is always around. Sometimes he fixes a stoop or returns a beer to the ice bucket. But mostly he waits for her. His name is Roderigo. They talk with their heads close together like lovers in the movies.

A little more than a week later Uncle starts coming. He arrives alone without Benya, and never offers to drive me home. The crowd of dark Cuban builders with tools parts as he passes. Everybody calls him *Señor*, even if we are all Communist and equal now. Gordana is impressed. I notice he too relishes her big nipples.

Soon she no longer talks sweetly to Roderigo. She is nice to me when Uncle is around. When he leaves she acts like I don't exist. She tells others she always knew she was worth noticing, even if she is poor, her father a dirt-covered miner and her mother a nothing. A girl like her is destined to marry somebody important with his own American car and an important job, somebody everybody calls *Señor*. He promised he'd leave his wife and his idiot daughter.

He says that to every girl, I want to tell her, upset she called Juma an idiot. The Party would never allow him to leave

Aunt Ludmila, daughter of a war hero, close confidant of Tito. I decide not to speak. She'll find out soon enough, like all the ballerinas and actresses who caught Uncle's eye before her.

In the beginning Gordana and Uncle are careful. She sneaks first into the janitor's room nobody uses. He enters behind her. Later they both come out a minute or two apart. He looks the same. Her hair is a little messier. Then they become sloppier, careless. The zipper on her skirt stays open and the color of his cheeks matches her blush. *Puta,* I want to call him.

There are yellow and white flowers, Uncle's favorite, on the stage the day before the weekend break. Gordana throws her choir cloak off. Her pretty arms gesture, I'll be back in a few days, to Roderigo. He saddens with disappointment; she slips into the front seat of our Ford. The car drives away, the space between her and Uncle's heads narrowing. I sit down and wait. One of the stage builders, the one with the hump in the middle of his back, walks over and whispers to Roderigo. He kicks the ice bucket, yelling, *Puta, puta.* Then he sits down in the middle of the slush and seems lost.

Only diplomats can buy Coke. It comes all the way from Germany. I bring a can to him and offer a sip. He looks up at me, at the can, at my pretty dress, and then at his friends, who are laughing, *Vendetta, vendetta.* I know they are coaxing him to revenge his honor but I don't care. Being close to him makes me forget all of them, everything.

· · ·

Every day I steal money and food, cans of ham, expensive French cheese, half-empty jugs of wine left over from our dinners. Lupe knows what I am doing. She tells me, I will cover for you. I give her a big hug and run outside into the shade under a mango tree where he waits.

At first we just ride our bikes. He leads. I follow far behind. He brings along a bruise-colored blanket.

Playa?

Sí.

The ocean is loud and we are alone. We sit for a while and listen. Then he lays me down on my back and spreads my legs, like Cousin, except gently.

Are you hurting, *mi amor?*

I know what he is asking me and I am not about to admit I am not. So I cry as if I were, and he relaxes and is happier than he would be if he knew someone else had hurt me before him. Gordana is prettier, and has big nipples, and if I didn't have something better than her, all the coupons and ham in the world wouldn't help.

We hide. We look for a different place, somewhere we haven't been yet. Always carrying the same blanket. The canal, the cane fields, the back of his friend's house where every gutter leaks. We return to the beach. The hot wind blows over the dunes when it's not raining and rolls the dry seaweed in front of us. If we are alone, he washes me in the water after. If the salt burns between my legs, he blows on it like Mother did when I was very small and I had a cut that needed to be washed out with alcohol. Sometimes he brings an empty beer bottle filled with fresh water and then it doesn't burn.

Blow on it anyway, I say.

Do you like it?

I like it a lot when it doesn't hurt.

How long will you be in Cuba? he asks me after a month as he kisses my forehead.

I pull away from being treated like a child.

A year, maybe.

And then?

Home, I guess.

You will leave me?

I don't know.

If you do, I will curse you.

I thought it's against the Party to curse, I say.

He doesn't answer for a while and I forget the question.

The Party, he finally says.

I see he is afraid to say more.

I don't know anything about your family, I say.

The story follows. His father was a famous drummer, left his mother when they were little. She worked in the factory, fending alone for her hungry children. He is proud of her. And loves her. He makes a strange face when I tell him Mother left Father. A woman to leave a man? He's never heard of such a thing. What kind of men do we breed in the cold country? Not real men, for sure. He turns his brown back away from me. Only weaklings are left behind by their wives. Your father must have been a softy man, a woman.

I am mad at him for saying such things about my dad, and I tell him he would never be able to come to the house, and how Uncle says the darkies are obstacles for Cuba, lazy, useless, promiscuous.

Now he is angry, and tells me he came only because I

am rich and have coupons and how I would never forget him because he was my first, and he would forget me as soon as he turned his back. I laugh. Oh, I'd forget. He was not my first. Men have wasted my time before. I see I have injured him, but I continue. Gordana rides in our Ford every day, sits in the front seat while Uncle has his fingers under her black skirt. She lets him, she lets an old wrinkled man touch her like that for chocolate and a drive in a fancy new car. Uncle even asked about the young darky rumored to have been her lover. How could you even ask? she frowned. How can anyone like a man darker than this chocolate, and she waved the bar in front of him. Uncle apologized for insulting her and took her to the Tropicana show, the most famous show in Havana, where poor people like Roderigo cannot afford to go to.

He is on top of me again, stronger, like Cousin now, forcing my arms back, legs apart, and he is crying *Puta, puta* and I am crying *Te amo* and he bites my skin, but then he kisses me, I am sorry, I am sorry, and then there is more pleasure than ever.

.   .   .

I am bleeding. There are stains on my underwear, brown and pasty, like espresso pudding. I don't know what it is. I bled once before, the first time Cousin hurt me. This could be the monthly thing I heard about. The thing that washes out a woman. But it could be something else, something to do with Roderigo. I can't ask. I sneak into Uncle's room and steal several socks. I use one at a time to keep the pudding from spreading. I throw the socks in the public wastebasket at night when I go on my bike ride.

I don't tell anyone. Those are my secrets. The socks, Roderigo, all of it. But the rumors have their own way of accumulating and spreading. Slowly at first. The gardener trimming the bushes in the middle of the night to avoid a vicious sun sees a black shadow sliding under the mango tree. He keeps it to himself at first. Then he sees it again. Tells the cleaning lady, The young mistress is into voodoo. Voodoo, she mocks. She is into what every hot little rich *puta* in this part of the world wants. A negrito. I turn up her unmade bed every morning. No voodoo keeps a girl from sleeping.

I hear a rumble of voices in the kitchen one night. Concerned voices.

It's a disease. It's wrong. I recognize the gardener's nasal singsong. A rich white girl and a poor black boy.

Certainly not a new story, Lupe objects. But I worry. She's not fifteen yet, won't be until the fall. Her mother should get her out of here.

One of the men should warn the boy, the gardener says. So he doesn't end up in more trouble than he can handle. What he's doing is crazy. The Party would never allow the marriage.

Marriage? Lupe's angry voice shakes the kitchen walls. What are you talking about? She's not fifteen!

I ignore the rumors. Mother asks nothing. She spends less time at home. She seems tired and pale. I wonder if being around Fidel wears her out. Roderigo wants me to come and meet his family, wants to meet Mother. When I tell him no his eyes are full of tears. Then I tell him, Next time, and he holds me, his body tense and distant as if he knows I am lying.

. . .

Three days before school starts, Uncle bursts into my bedroom and grabs me—you little slut—by the hair and throws me on the floor. My head hits the upholstered edge of the chair. I almost laugh, It didn't hurt, at him.

Ludmila holds Mother back at the door. Uncle kicks me, and I crunch up in a ball. Then Cousin Juma jumps at Aunt Ludmila, and Mother twists away and tackles Uncle. Stop it, she screams. He turns around and clutches her hands: Dear, dear, you shouldn't be here, you should be in bed, you are terribly sick, my dear. He turns to me: Look what you did to your mother, she is sick, sick because of you, her womb is killing her, the womb she carried you in, you no-good whore, see how pale she is. Stop it, she whispers. Don't tell me not to tell her, he hollers, she should know what she's done. Your mother is dying, you terrible, terrible little slut!

I can smell the rum on his breath, and I know he is drunk, and I am hurting everywhere, and Cousin Juma is screaming, screaming, hitting herself on the face, scratching herself, and her arms are bleeding. Daddy, stop, stop, please, she cries. He stops only because he is tired. He looks at me, tells me, You make me sick, you make everyone sick, and he leaves the room.

Minutes pass before anyone speaks. Mother sits on the floor with her face down. Aunt Ludmila is leaning against the door holding on to the frame. Cousin Juma is on the floor licking her bleeding forearms and humming. Mother crawls over to her and touches her head.

That's a pretty song, sweetheart, she says.
Uh-huh.

Don't do that—she moves Juma's mouth from her arm—
it'll get infected.

I sit in the corner and nobody looks at me.

. . .

It's official by the next afternoon—we are leaving. Somebody
has packed our bags, piled neatly by the door, and we are
flying in the morning. They thought I would fight and scream,
but I am just sitting down in my room. Someone carries our
bags to the car and loads it. The hood screeches as they force
it closed. I write silly things on a piece of paper, trying to
phrase a good-bye to Lupe, to Benya, to Roderigo, but I don't
know what to say.

I go over to Juma's room. She is bobbing on the bed,
repeating, Sorry-sorry, Sorry-sorry. I take my brush out of
my purse. It's old and scratched and not at all as elegant as
Mother's. I offer my best pins. She accepts.

Pretty, I whisper. She likes it when I call her pretty.
Listen to me, I say.

She draws near and tunes in to me.

You are not as stupid as they think. Just don't drink
any of their tea and lemonade. That's what makes you
stupid.

She drops her chin lower.

I mean it, I say and turn toward the door.

Sasha, she calls.

I stop. Our eyes lock.

Thank you.

. . .

Aunt Ludmila leads me to make sure there is no scene and mutters, Please be quiet in front of the help. We have been embarrassed enough by your shenanigans with the poor darkie boyfriend. The shame could get all the way to the Central Committee, all the way to Tito's ears. It could ruin us all. I nod obediently. Lupe touches my arm as I walk by, but it takes everything I have in my legs to continue. Benya is not driving, Uncle is. Mother hides her eyes from me, and I stumble humbly into the car.

· · ·

The flight back is long and the stewardesses are nice. They know we are related to somebody important; they saw the car was allowed all the way to the plane escalator. Mother sits all the way in the front, away from me.

We break in Prague in the transit hotel near the airport. Mother goes to bed without coming down to lunch. At least here in Prague we can mingle with people, she says. Here our passports are good enough for mixing in. We don't have to sleep hunched over in the airport seat with our heads in our hands like we had to in Canada, where people from Communist countries are not like other respectable citizens.

She says she doesn't want to leave the room until dinner, and will I go to that nice lady at the gift desk to buy a watch for Mother's youngest sister?

I promised her a Bulova, she says.

I have never been entrusted with such a task, and I buy the watch that costs exactly as much as I have in my hands. A watch is a watch, what do I know? I think nervously of Mother in the bed upstairs. A young Czech woman with skin even paler than Mother's wraps the round Bulova with Roman numbers inside a square box.

Mother wakes up for dinner and, sick or not, she is still lovely in her claret dress. The hotel manager walks up to us instantly.

Please, follow me, he says.

He serves us beluga and bread and butter himself. I ask for mango, and both he and Mother give me the what-is-wrong-with-you look, you strange girl, asking for mango in landlocked Czechoslovakia. Don't you know this is Europe?

I push the food around my plate.

Why aren't you eating? It is the first question Mother has asked me in months.

Not hungry.

Don't worry. She touches me gently, the way Lupe touched Kotorita. It will pass. Everything passes quickly when you're young.

I look down at the table.

Back in the room she tumbles onto the bed, exhausted again.

You can lie down next to me if you want, she says.

I cuddle next to her and hold her tight.

Are you hurting from Uncle Malik? she asks.

No. I'm just afraid.

Of what?

I don't know.

She kisses me.

We lie in silence as the planes roar over our transit room. The runway lights are blue and red and orange. They flicker over the thin blanket that covers her body.

What is Father like? I ask after a while.

She turns onto her back. The orange light falls on her face. She looks healthy that way.

I didn't know him very well, she says.

Aunt Dika says he's a liar.

Everybody has an opinion.

Dika doesn't lie.

Everybody lies.

She closes her eyes slowly and it seems like she is asleep. I wait. Her chest moves slowly up and down for a while as the fourth plane whistles outside. I return to my bed.

Make sure you are covered well, she says with her eyes closed. This is not Cuba.

I sneak under the blanket and the sheets are cold and I wonder how many people have slept on them, and were they as unhappy as Mother is, and were they as scared as I am, and were they pretending to sleep although the clocks are upside down and it's only lunchtime in Havana.

Mother turns onto her hip. The blanket falls into the crescent of her waist. Her breathing changes, gets faster. I think she's crying. I hug her again. She seems thinner than a minute ago. I kiss her the way she used to kiss me when I was little and she thought I was sleeping, on the back of my head right where the hair disappears into the neck.

Sleep, *Mamita.* I call her the same way the little Cubans call their mommas. She is relaxing. I whisper, I too left my heart in Cuba, but she says nothing and she just shakes a little with muted sobs. Don't worry, I tell her, I am here. *Guantanamera*, I sing, *guajira guantanamera, no se preocupe, niña, te amo, te amo, te amo.*

4

The sunny and dry weather lifts the heavy
burden of our return. My hair flattens, but
I am happy to see the large people with
broad faces and shoulders who remind
me of myself. Mother's in the front seat,
straight-backed and taut as if a grave pain
pushes from the inside. I sit in the back
next to Aunt Dika.

Look at the crows pecking at something dead, Mother
points out.

Their plumage is glowing blackness. Beautiful like dark
eagles or falcons, they shriek and loop around the carcass
with precision and grace. I envy the birds.

It's probably a dead cat. Don't look at it, Dika soothes.

No, it's a dead crow, Mother decides. They're eating their
own.

Maybe it's sleeping, and they are trying to wake it, I say.

Yes, maybe, Mother whispers.

I try sliding my hand under Aunt Dika's fingers, but her hand is pressed hard into the seat, her gaze interlocked with the landscape speeding outside the car window. The hurt, some strange hurt only brave adults are privy to, pales her lips and neck. I want to talk, but I am too afraid.

. . .

My bedroom is strange. The familiar things remain the same; the white and gray streaks on my piano, my cold blond dolls. But they are smaller, as if they belonged to somebody slighter, narrower. I open the drawers of my desk and spy on myself. Neat, pretty things, new notebooks with empty stickers that await the fall semester, expensive napkins I snatched from some hotel. Underneath, a mess: clips, papers, notes. In this drawer I am a typical boring girl. I jostle the drawer in with my fingers caught and wait until I have to let go.

Cool air carrying the tinges of pine and beef stew streams though the window, strange to me. A woman yells out in a guttural voice that resonates the same as mine. Deep and harsh. No more of Lupe's melodious singing. A child cries out. That sound is always the same.

. . .

The doctors, many doctors, appear. They are humble in our prominent house. At our door, their doctor's privileges cease. One cannot condescend in the house of a very sick relative of someone connected to the Party. I hide behind the door to watch.

Open the window, the tallest, most important doctor suggests. The patient needs fresh air.

The curtain twists as they converse, consult, and clang their metal, medicinal tools. Mother is laid flat on her back. The tall doctor, cloaked in an air of concentration, slinks on a pair of gloves and approaches the patient. The other two lift her legs up, spread them. The tall doctor takes a long pointy thing and pokes about her inside. She cries, Please, a little easier, please.

I lunge at the doctor, grab him by the hand, and yank his weapon away. Leave her, leave her, and the other two doctors grab me, and Aunt Dika is yelling, What is the matter with you now? Do you want her to die like this? Go to your room and stay there until somebody calls you.

I don't want to go. I'll be good, please, I say, let me stay. But Aunt pushes me away. The others huddle around Mother, who is still on her back, and I can't see her face as they close the door.

My bedroom door thumps shut behind me. I am on the ground and the key clicks. Now I am alone. I slam against the wall my room shares with Mother's. I hit it again and again and there is Dika's screaming outside the door, Stop it, stop it, you lunatic. We are going to send you away, you rotten girl. Then there is a feeble knock on the wall and I think I can hear Mom saying, Please be good, and I want to but I don't know how. I am the worst girl who has ever lived and how can she ask me to be good, how can she ask the worst girl to do anything other than to be the worst?

. . .

Dika knocks hours later. There is a phone call for you. Her voice is somber. It is the tone she uses for describing the great battles against the Nazis and their collaborators when she distinguished herself and earned her many shiny medals. I emerge with my head down and answer.

Alexandra, it's Dad.

I am surprised to hear my full name, surprised to hear Father's voice. The family refers to him as a sperm donor. He never calls.

Are you there? he asks.

Yes.

Mother and I decided you should come and spend some time with me. She is not feeling well, and needs to rest.

Father smells of unaired clothes hung near the stove where something putrid, like old mutton and pickled cabbage, boiled for hours. I overheard Mother say she was sick every time he touched her, and how he left a dirty stain on his side of the bed. I pull away as far as I can in the car. His nose has a forward bump like mine. His upper lip is tight and turned inward.

I don't want to leave Momma, I say.

Fine, he answers. We'll go for a short drive, and then we'll take you back home.

He pulls over in front of a children's department store. While he is flirting with the salesgirl, who tells me I look just like my father, he piles jeans, undershirts, shirts, socks, underwear, and two bathing suits on the counter. He jots her phone number on the receipt. In case he has some more questions about the children's clothes, he says. She is always home after six, she says, to check on her sick grandmother.

How proper, Father commends. I'll be sure not to call before seven, then.

He carries my bags toward the car, suddenly in a good mood, and when I ask him for whom he got all those clothes, he grunts, When did you get so snoopy and start taking after your two no-good aunts, and why do you always have to be so difficult, and if you must know, I wanted to make a sale, a commission, for the poor girl.

Commission?

Sure, he says.

Isn't the point of Communism that there are no more commissions and that everybody is supposed to do the best they can without incentive?

Which idiot taught you that? he asks.

My teachers. I knew mentioning Aunts and Uncles would only irritate him more.

It would be the point if the goddamn peasant who took over the country, like your half-wit uncles and their retarded offspring, could run anything other than maybe a pigsty. I did it for that girl. And why don't you shut up?

So I do.

He pulls over at the gas station and fills up the car for a lot of money, and when the attendant asks if the trip is long he says, Very.

I panic. He is taking me away. I wrap my fingers around the door handle, but I'm afraid to open it.

We stop by Father's last wife's place and my little half brother jumps into the backseat. Father smiles at him and kisses him. Calls him baby. He loves him. In Greece, where Father and his last wife lived for the two years they were married, people call him Arapaki, little Arab, because he tans like I do. They like it on him. He is a boy, which is better no matter what color.

Arapaki asks to go to a merry-go-round. Let's go, let's go, around and around, let's go, let's go. Father turns around and tickles him. I'll give you a merry-go-round right here.

I see my chance. Yes, please, please, let's go to the park, I plead.

He looks at me and the smile fades. You too?

Yes, yes!

Yes, yes! from the backseat.

The park is filled with children with parents, young lovers, and groups of old ladies with purple hair. Father gives me the money to buy tickets and he turns to show my half brother the go-carts, something he can ride next year. When is the next year, the son asks, tomorrow? No, silly, the loving father answers and pulls his son back to his chest. It's next year.

I think of Roderigo across the world, and how I will never see him, not tomorrow, not next year, not ever, and of Mother and the dark secret living inside of her, and I crumple the money in my palm and run.

I run. I run as fast as I can, and it's easy this time. Natural. I am not scared, not scared at all. I take off my shoes, one in each hand, not to be heard or followed. I run over prickly pebbles, over shiny train tracks, a lost key, past yogurt cartons, a confused cat, a couple concealed by the shrubs, a school yard, until my chest is burning and I stop.

What's the rush? a young soldier leaning against a wall outside a bar asks me.

I don't answer. I hear the off-key wailing of a singer inside.

Do you want a drink? He motions with his glass.

I take his glass and throw a drink down like a man. My throat is hot, but I like it.

Nobody is coming after you, he says. If they were, they'd be here already.

How do you know? I ask.

It's the kind of thing soldiers know.

What's it like, being a soldier? I ask.

Easy, he says and blows smoke in a coil. You just have to tell the truth.

Mother's friend lives close by the amusement park. I hope she'll help me. I knock at the door and wait. She opens and scans me without a hello. She is also a close friend of Aunt Ludmila, and I can see she's heard the unimaginable thing about me, about the poor Cuban, the disgrace. Come in the kitchen, she tells me, straight to the kitchen, away from her fine carpets, with those filthy bleeding feet. I lift my feet up and lean them against the chair legs so as not to make more mess.

She says she'll call Mother, let her know I am safe, and make me some tea. She even asks what kind I like, chamomile or mint.

Anything, please, I say. I don't want to be a bother.

Then the police show up, and as she sees them out she preaches on the importance of fathers and husbands and respect for the family.

* * *

Mother is on her bed facing the wall. Aunt Dika walks in behind me.

There she is, she says.

I sit and wait. Mother turns around.

What's wrong with your feet? she asks.

I cut them running.

Better wash them with warm water.

Okay.

Step on the towel and make sure they are dry before you put on your socks so they don't get infected.

Okay.

Then Father bangs at the door. We better let him in, he roars. This is his child they are turning against him, he has the right. He pushes Aunt Dika out of his way, ignores me, stops in front of Mother, and spits.

You whore, you started this, he says. This is all your fault. And now she is fit for the street.

He just stands there shaking with rage. Mother turns back to the wall. Aunt Dika is in a panic about the crazy half-Gypsy loose in the house. Somebody please help us, the three help-less creatures, one sick, one with a bullet in her leg, and one a crazy little girl. Ah, if only she didn't have the German present lodged in her bone she'd show him a lesson. Nobody notices I've gone to the kitchen and have taken the knife out of the cupboard. I grasp the handle as tightly as I can.

I am not yet fifteen and the blade of the knife I am holding is pressed against Father's back, and Mother is staring at the wall.

Get out of our house, I whisper.

The numbed sound of my voice stuns him.

I am your father, he says, all the fury deflated.

Get out of my house, I say.

Defeated Father leaves the room. He passes my blue-eyed cousin, my gaping uncle. The two have just arrived after Uncle's concerned friend, the police inspector, left a discreet message saying the entire affair, as unpleasant as it was, could be removed from the girl's record. All it would take was one word from Uncle's outstanding mouth. I swing the blade in front of the blue eyes and Cousin squeals like a stray. My lungs swell with pride. I squeeze the handle in my hand all night and nobody, not Dika, not Cousin, not even Mother, comes to my room.

. . .

After an emergency family council I am informed that the good sages of our family have decided to send me off to the mountains of western Bosnia to stay with my senile grandmother. There is no trouble she can get herself into over there, Dika says, that place is so far away from everything, and there is a young keeper staying with Grandmother who will keep an eye on her. At dusk Mother knocks on my door and asks to come in.

She is wearing her purple robe and she looks pretty. I sit up on my bed without lifting my face, my heart racing.

How are you? she asks.

Fine.

You made everyone mad with this last one.

I know.

Why did you run?

I don't know.

Something must've set you off.

Are you really sick? I ask. I heard them talking about you being sick.

I'm sick, but I'm getting better.

Sure?

Yes. So please go to Grandma and try to be good, be a girl again, and I'll try to get better quickly.

. . .

Later in life that would be the image of Mother I'd remember the most often. Her purple robe, the one she insisted on wearing up until her death. It was still new. Her hair was still in place. Her face unbloated.

In my memory she never gets old. She is younger than I am now. I fight the disease that accelerated her death by ignoring it. She keeps her beauty, one thing she had more than anyone else. In my memory she is intact.

I might have had a chance to speak to her that night. Ask her questions. She was vulnerable and frightened. She might have given something away. But I let it pass. I passed up the chance to become like many women I know who have mothers, aging mothers, wise mothers who listen and understand. Average mothers I forget as soon as I walk away from their average tables. Long ago I decided to keep Mother at her best—proud, beautiful, and distant.

She lied that day. I think I knew. Or maybe I felt it without seeing, as children often do. There could have been many reasons for her lying, none of which I would know for sure.

Not that I haven't tried to figure it out. That day would turn me into someone who diligently practices unearthing liars, and their motivation. I became a Specialist. But I left the lie she told me alone. For Mother and me, it was our cloak-and-dagger, our mystery. We never told. We never asked. Her Cancer, my Secrets—our Pact.

5

My breath is frosty here at night even in
August. The house is old. Hundreds of
years old. Cobblestones line the entrance
path, which is perpetually muddy and
stalls even the lightest of wheelbarrows.
Square broad walls circle a wide hearth
with a slowly sinking chimney. The hearth
is always lit and the house glows orange
through the windows at night. The
neighbors soothe their freezing fingers
on the warm stone when they visit.
Memories are heavy in this house. Of births, of deaths,
wars, truces. Of the eldest son who took over the first floor
after he was married. Of the second-born who moved into the
narrower upstairs quarters. The rest tried their luck on the
merchant ships. At Christmas or Ramadan they wrote from
faraway places and asked about old loves and aging parents.

Those who stayed built smaller, cheaper houses with no proper foundations. Inevitably some harsh Bosnian blizzard tore the feeble building down and the whole process started anew.

Nobody really remembers where the generations of girls ended up, unless they made favorable matches, and then people recalled the lands, the barns, the houses where they bore their sons. All I ever heard of my maternal great-grandmother was that she had golden hair braided in twists thick as a man's arm. They made her famous among suitors throughout five counties. She had fourteen children, nine boys.

I have a friend here. Frances. Named after a patron saint of her Catholic house. Speckle-faced, like a cuckoo's egg, Mother once joked. It stuck. She is the only one who knows about Cousin. Last year, we were huddled in bed together, her russet freckles facing my black eyes, when she asked me if I had ever seen it. I made her lean so close that I could smell the ground sugar we stole from the kitchen for dessert on her face. I whispered my secret.

No! She leaped on all fours like a dog and bobbed her forehead against my chest.

Yes!

We growled for a while, wrestled and guffawed, and finally she grew serious and said, That's a mortal sin.

You get used to it after a while, I said.

Hush your dirty mouth. She yanked me off the bed. On your knees. Let's pray.

To whom? I asked.

To Jesus.

To Jesus, I laughed. Why him?

He helps.

Didn't help me.

Did you ask?

No.

There you go.

We kneeled and prayed and I went home at the end of August. She hugged me strongly at the bus station, told me she loved me, and rushed back home so as not to be late for the evening milking.

. . .

Frances's entire family swarms me at Grandmother's front door before my bags hit the floor. The girls enter, the boys stay out. The rules haven't changed since last year. Nothing ever changes here.

Sasha Sasha, the smallest girls coo as we kiss.

Frances is almost seventeen! She is engaged! the second oldest exclaims, breathless with excitement. Everybody calls her Cheery for her perpetual grin and the deep-pitted dimples she wears every day.

Frances is rounder. The last year has erased most of her uneven brownness. She is calm and lovely. The poise with which she holds her youngest sisters in check, There, there, be quiet, while smiling, suddenly reminds me of Mother.

Welcome, Alexandra, she whispers serenely.

Alexandra! Cheery mocks and elbows her. Listen to her! Ever since the baker's son promised to take her off our father's back she's gotten her snout up in the air.

Keep your voice down, Frances says.

See? What'd I tell you? Cheery laughs. Right up there, tearing the clouds.

What's all this commotion, Mina? Mina, Grandmother calls from her bedroom. It's not the Germans or the Catholics?

She has forgotten everything she has known, other than the big war, and is now convinced I am Mina, her youngest, the one killed in the elevator accident the first year after the family moved to the big city. I walk into her room quietly. She is coiled inside a window seat, two feet off the floor, ancient and sagging as this house. Her white hair is up in a few-days-old bun and her housedress almost clean.

Hello, I say.

Who is it? The blank, frightened eyes are intent.

It's the good neighbors, the Communist's children. Don't worry. We are going out to play.

I walk over to her, sneaking Aunt Ludmila's lipstick from my pocket. Grandma's keeper is away until later, and I can do what I want.

What's that? she asks.

To make you beautiful.

I can't be. She pulls a handful of her skin away from her face. The wrinkles stretch out like an old stocking. I am old.

You are to me.

You were always such a good daughter.

I roll the color over her shrinking mouth. The thin whiteness clashes with the lipstick's redness as if she's bit through her lips and is bleeding slowly. Grandma's skin has never been out in the sun. I wipe it off.

I'm sorry, she says.

Come on, come on, Cheery urges from the other room. Mother is anxious to see you.

I place a quick kiss on her stale-smelling shoulder and run my hand over the white hair.

I'll be back soon.

Watch out for the elevators, she whispers.

. . .

I steal a jar of peach jam from the cupboard to take as a gift, since I brought nothing, and one cannot go for a visit after a long time with empty hands like some sort of a wild hoodlum, I remember from childhood instructions. We leave my bags and run. Frances's house is small. A puny shack with a concrete floor, housing the ten children, their mother, and their father. It belonged to my family before the war. After the Communists won and the nationalization started, Uncles publicly gave it away to the people, claiming we needed it much less. A much smarter act than to have it confiscated and get shot, as often happened after the Reds tried the bourgeois criminals.

We stack up on the sofa and wait for their mother, Mila, to start talking. She looks me up and down, wraps her shawl tighter, and lights a cigarette. Mila was once pretty, with reddish hair, a smooth face and straight nose, no freckles or other blemishes. The daughters inherited those from their father. Beauty is a lot to be proud of even if a woman is poor. But all her land would have been mine if it wasn't for the Revolution and it shames her. She never talks to me without thinking first.

I suppose you heard about the engagement, she says proudly.

I nod.

Our family has greatly benefited from this match. She exhales. Show Sasha the presents we receive daily, she tells Frances.

Frances returns with a wicker basket in her hands. She lifts the rag used to ward off hungry horseflies.

There. See?

The bread smells fresh.

His father sends a loaf every morning, Mila says. Two big ones and a dry cake on Sundays.

A dry cake, the little boys laugh. Dry cake.

She pops the jam jar. The five youngest rush to the table. Their chubby fingers dip in and Mila scorns, Eat like civilized children, slow down, slow down. They plead, More, more, knowing the best time to ask for a second helping is in front of visitors, since no one would ever admit to not having enough in front of guests. Especially if the guest's family once owned everything they have. So they get their second and third helpings and stick their little fingers in the jar until their faces, ears, and hair are covered with jam and we are all laughing. Mila's smile fades the quickest. I tell her about Cuban mango to cheer her up, and how they dance in the street on Fat Tuesday.

I don't believe it! She fixes her shawl again. On the street? Not Catholics, I am sure.

All Catholics. But in secret.

In secret?

Yes, the Party over there won't let them.

Ah, the Party, she mutters and draws an imaginary line on the floor with her toe.

Roderigo said the same about the Party.

Who's Roderigo?

My friend, the Catholic whose father the drummer left him when he was a baby with two brothers and sisters. His mother worked in the factory to feed them.

God bless her soul, Frances said. He sounds nice.

His skin was chocolate color, like all your freckles together.

Frances's mother sits up straight as an arrow. My child, do you know a black man?

I pause.

He's Catholic, just like you, is the first thing I can think of.

They are savages, she murmurs in fear. People eaters.

What's people eaters? Frances's youngest brother asks.

The blacks. Already burnt by the flames of hell.

Burnt? The boy yelps.

Yes, like you'll be on the Judgment Day for not finishing your peas at lunch, Mila scoffs.

I don't like peas.

Nothing but peas in hell, she threatens. Here you only get them twice a week, but there you'll be eating peas every day and be burnt black like charcoal.

The little face grimaces, he is about to cry, and the older brother jumps and tickles the little body, chanting, The burnt man, the burnt man is coming. He'll fly through the windows and scorch the curtains, and eat you first because you're the sweetest with jam on your face and your head.

Mila blesses herself at the thought of a burnt man, and

nothing will stop the youngest from crying. Not even his mother wringing the older brother's ears until he apologizes. The burnt man will get me, the burnt man is coming, he'll eat me first with jam, with jam, and he won't shut up until there is a bottle in his mouth and he is in his cradle.

See what you did, with your slick city-mouth, Mila scorns me.

Sorry, I say.

She looks at me the way Dika does when she knows I am lying.

Frances faintly rocks her head toward the door, and I get up and excuse myself.

Thank you, I say. I have to go and see about Grandma.

Too bad she's turned dim, Mila says triumphantly. But that happens so much in your family.

That's what happens when you own everybody's land for generations, I retaliate. Everybody has to pay for what they have. That's why your kids are all healthy. Except for the dead one, of course.

Mila's eyes change. Her firstborn was retarded from birth and died before his first birthday. The doctors blamed the nearby factory for polluting the water. For peasants it was different. All abnormalities were the mother's fault.

Frances pushes me toward the door.

Don't talk like that to my mother, she whispers.

She started it.

That doesn't matter. It's not right, and she's bound to forbid us to talk to you.

That would be terrible. Would it make her feel better if I went to Mass with you on Sunday?

Are you joking?

No.

Muslims don't go to Mass.

I'd go to shut her up.

I guess it wouldn't hurt.

We stand in the chilly air and I wonder how many more times we'll be able to talk like this. The wedding is set for the next Christmas.

So you liked it when he touched you? she asks.

How do you know I liked it?

I know.

How?

You seem different.

I was always different.

Different different. How was it?

Better than when Cousin did it.

We both grow quiet. The night is quickly taking over the mountain, erasing the sounds of the day.

I just can't imagine, she says. A cousin? Every family's got a bad apple. My uncle's a pig like that. He'd do something awful for sure. I just keep him too drunk for damage when he's around girls.

I wish I could get everybody in my family drunk, so they'd leave me alone, I say.

Maybe I could give you some of my father's brandy, she jokes. Put it in the soup. Except this year's might kill them instead. Too much rain soaked the plums and we had to bake them twice as long. It burns like the flames of hell Mother always talks about.

Even better, I say.

We laugh. Every summer it takes us a day or two to adjust, figure out what the other one has been doing. This year we are close quickly.

Silently, we sit on the concrete slab underneath the open gate.

How did you stop yourself from getting pregnant? she asks me.

I don't know. I did nothing.

Girls have to be careful. Guys won't. We have to keep away from their thing. The nuns told us a girl could get pregnant from the boy's thing touching any place on our bodies.

What do nuns know?

Even Selma, one of the girls who knows such things, said it's especially lethal near your belly button. That's how babies are fed in the belly. It's cut after they are born.

I had a crusty belly button as a baby, I remember. Mother told me there was a wound there for more than a month.

Then you must have bad luck. You shouldn't even step in the shower after a man. That alone can catch you a baby.

Whoever told you that is some idiot, I say. You have to have the thing inside your legs and they have to spill their water in your eggs.

Eggs? There are eggs inside a person?

Tiny eggs.

Tiny? But we are bigger than chickens.

You've got a point there. Maybe theirs are bigger because we are not laid, we are born.

Maybe. And you know what else I heard? The Gypsies have more babies in them. Each time they have a baby it's actually two or three. Are your visits on time?

What visits?

From the Red Sea.

I have no idea what she is talking about and I look at her, scared.

Do you bleed every month? she explains.

Not every. Sometimes, but it's brown.

Jesus, then you are in trouble already.

What should I do?

Of all the sins you had to pick the most mortal of them all. She is terrified. What were you thinking?

We don't know for sure it's a baby.

Don't know? You go frolicking with your eggs in some foreign land with a burnt man who probably has more babies than the darkest of the Gypsies in his thing, and you tell me it's not for sure?

Now I'm panicked.

What should I do? I ask.

I don't know. I heard you can jump up and down near a well, and the power of the hole may drag out the baby.

The well?

Yes! Go, go quickly! Jump up and down with your legs spread until you are so tired you can't move anymore.

I rush under the dark moon wondering if the brown bleeding means I have a baby in my belly. My stomach is bulging from the baker's bread and cake sucking up the lemonade and growing. I can hardly see the well. The trees are in full bloom, heavy with leaves, and the woods are thick around me. I hear swooshing, creaking, bending, and then there is a cramp in my stomach like a small fist and a piece of cake comes back.

The well walls are only two feet off the ground. I push the cover off and see the moon drawing jittery lines at the water's sloshing surface. The cool air streams up.

Coo-coo, I say to the water.

Ooo-ooo comes back.

I stand up, spread my legs, and start to jump. I try to think of a song but I can't think and jump at the same time. The bread and lemonade press against my stomach and I am nauseous, but I keep bobbing and soon I am sweaty and my feet are sore; the wells are dug out in dense clay that hurts my knees, and the juice and bits of bread drown my throat and I spit.

Jig and hop all you want, little slut, Grandma's keeper speaks behind me. It won't help.

Her bedroom window overlooks the well, and I can see her shadow. Her family is poor, but they are Muslim, never part of the serfdom, and she likes to distinguish herself as superior. She struts around the village cursing at the Christian children, Shoo, little bastards, take your pig smell out of my way.

I say nothing. I don't have to talk to the poor employee if I don't want to.

Look at you, she sneers. Didn't even dry the city mud on your shoes before you came back to your roots, and already running to the Catholics.

They are my friends. Now I am mad, so I answer.

Friends? They've slaughtered more Muslims than Germans.

Those didn't.

No, not yet.

. . .

What was all that ruckus around the well about? she drills from the moment I enter the house. She is fatter than last year, and I am sure we are paying for it.

What ruckus? I ask.

Don't get smart with me, young hussy, you know what I'm asking you. And where is that jar that was in the cupboard?

No, I don't know what you are asking me. I stare at her. And I promise you I'm not trying to be smart. Actually, I'm stupid. Very stupid. So stupid, I forget where we keep the chocolate and butter. It seems we have none left. Maybe you could help me find it, or at least look for it, before I call home and tell them it's missing, that is, when you're done talking about the ruckus around the well.

She is mad I have found her out and clatters Grandmother's plates.

What is it? The Germans? Grandma calls from her bedroom.

Nothing, nothing, the keeper answers. I'm just getting you a drink, my dear. She disappears into the room with a glass of milk. We will never become friends, that's clear, but she will leave me alone.

.   .   .

I can't sleep. I think of Roderigo and Lupe and Mother and sit up in my bed. Grandmother calls. The keeper's room remains mute. She calls again. Pleads. I walk in to see what she needs. Her room smells of slow decaying, as if what is inside has stopped already, given up. I take the fresh quinces from the kitchen table and shove them under her bed. The young smell will return by the morning. I tuck them all the way up to the wall so the keeper won't find and eat them. Even last summer, Frances warned me the keeper's reputation was that of a thief. I smiled and told her there was nothing in the old house to steal. Make sure your grandmother, now back to being a baby, Frances said, God bless her purity, is fed in front of you. The keeper's family is rotten, and everybody knows this. We were going to call your aunts, but the no-good thief keeps the phone number to herself.

   . . .

Mother doesn't write. She calls a few times, but the nearest phone is far and the neighbors tell her I am away. The respectable village women do not want me around their homes, inside their kitchens. A no-good girl should be kept away from their daughters, their carpets, their sitting pillows. Rumor of the burnt man has spread. I have been touched before I was married, stained by a man, a foreigner, an infidel. The village deals with it the best they can. I am banned. Quietly. It's never said explicitly, my Uncles and Aunts are too important. I am simply never invited to participate in the hours of tobacco smoking, coffee drinking, and sitting cross-legged on the floor listening to the men discuss politics.

The lowly Christians are my option.

I bear my eradication cheerfully. Frances takes me to Mass, and I learn a pretty Catholic song, about the vastness of the sea, and make sure to sing it in front of the keeper every day.

I play soccer and go to the movies. Frances's twin brothers are sweet on me. Dome and Zdeno. Always together. Dome flunked a grade in the elementary school, and then Zdeno wouldn't hear of separating and would not be dragged inside the fourth-grade classroom. He stood clutching the doorway and screaming, Dome, Dome, come, until he was allowed back into the third grade. I make them fight over who gets to carry my bag, although I don't really care since they look exactly the same, blondish hair, bad teeth, and a river of freckles across their faces.

The premiere of a new movie is always a celebration. There is only one theater and during summers the movie changes every week. This week, it's Bruce Lee's *Enter the Dragon*. The boys are saying they've been waiting all their lives to see it.

I am usually the only girl to go. This time Frances says she might be able to sneak out. Her folks cracked opened the new barrel of brandy and soon they won't know what day it is. Whenever that happens they'll sleep through cannon fire. She'll leave Cheery to watch the rest of the kids. There is plenty of sugar and bread to keep the little mouths quiet should anyone wake up.

I have to help with milking before we go. Just as I sit under the cow, Frances enters the barn. She is grave and official.

Have you been jumping by the well? she asks.

Plenty, I say. Woke the old Allah up, and now you're my only friend.

Stop it with God. She frowns impatiently. So, you are not pregnant.

No. I squeeze on the teat hard, and the milk trickles.

I have something to tell you.

What? Are we in trouble for the movie?

No. Your mom has a dying disease in her belly, cancer.

How do you know? I squeeze harder until the cow twitches.

Everybody knows.

Did you get the tickets for the movie? I ask.

Yes, she whispers.

Good.

In front of the theater the Gypsy vendors fill their carts with fresh pumpkin and sunflower seeds. It is the same popcorn machine as last year, and its slow popping doesn't match the demand. The line is long.

This year there is an exciting addition. Pink cotton candy. The locals could only read about it before; it was reserved for the big cities and only for the days when the circus arrived. The older women gather around the strange machine in awe. They are skilled in the art of spinning, and they bless themselves thinking of the luxury of this invention. Some man was rich enough to be able to melt bags and bags of precious sugar in order to come up with this idea, one of them concludes. A miracle.

Although it's expensive, parents are buying it and the children are playing, fencing with it, until parts catch and there are cries, and snuffling noses, and I-hate-yous between friends, and the crafty mother's hand untangles the pink treasure and the friendships are renegotiated.

Mother has the most beautiful hands, I say to myself.

. . .

The movie is good and I eat popcorn and pumpkin seeds and sunflower seeds and two cotton candies and I am still hungry, hungry, and I am afraid of cancer and what it will do to Mother's hands, and I wish I was Bruce Lee, who beats everybody bad and evil, kicks them hard, but I cannot and I have some more popcorn until I feel calmer.

After the movie the whole town walks up and down the main street, cleared for pedestrians. People come from deep in the forest, from up the mountains and down the hunting paths to show off their best clothes, their best animals, their prettiest daughters. Boys look. The girls humbly drop their glances. Parents strike bargains. Matches are made.

I watch their to-and-fro and wish I was one of them. If Mother wasn't sick, terribly sick, facing the wall, we too could be here now, posing, flaunting our respectable colors, looking for a young man whose parents would think it an honor to receive a girl from such a good family.

Let's go and steal somebody's potatoes, I suggest to the twins.

No, it's dangerous, Frances warns, mad at me for suggesting.

Danger is good, the twins say.

I am not back in bed for more than two hours when a long tree branch hits me across the calves. Dome is reaching through the window bars toward the bottom of my bed, whispering, Get up, get up, you no-good city-sloth, the Steneks' potatoes are waiting.

What? I can hardly open my eyes.

We are getting into the old man's potatoes tonight, the whole gang is. It was your idea. You'll be a traitor if you don't come.

I throw my clothes out first and sneak through the middle bar slightly wider on one side, bent for the purpose of sneaking out for generations, and kick Dome after he says, Your ass almost got stuck. I clutch my sneakers as we are crawling under the keeper's window, and when we are free and clear about eighty feet away we slap each other on our palms like the famous basketball players do on TV.

You slap hard like a man, he says.

Why haven't they sent you to the army and court-martialed you yet? I ask.

No, next year. When I'm done with high school.

You'll be twenty-five by the time you finish.

Take this. He tosses a jute bag at me. You'll be the collector. I shove it under my shirt, determined not to scratch like a city-baby, no matter how much the jute burns my naked skin.

We cross the river under the white moon, and it's freezing and we are laughing at Zdeno, who slides over a slippery rock, because he is dumb enough not to take his shoes off and feel the bottom with his bare feet.

Fuck you all, he scoffs as he wipes his dripping face. I'd rather be all wet than touch something awful with my bare feet like a snake or a bloodsucker.

I am not afraid of the river snakes. I know they are more afraid of us. But the bloodsuckers scare me, and I hurry through the rocks to the other side. We make it quickly under the barbed wire and start digging for potatoes.

Dummy, Dome calls to me. Don't take any puny ones hard enough to crack your teeth. Then you'll look like your grandmother.

I know he means well. He leers at me the same way Roderigo did. I know I can get him to do whatever I want him to do, so I decide he'll be the one carrying the sack home.

Then a clap of thunder louder than any I heard in Cuba flies above our heads. Dome drops flat on his belly right next to me cursing, Shit, shit, the old man is not asleep. We are going to lose our goddamn heads over some fucking potatoes that aren't even that good.

Thunder again, and by now even I know the old man Stenek, on one of his insomniac stretches, is shooting at us.

Get lost! Dome commands.

We run across the stream to safety, Zdeno holding on to the potato sack, all wet and freezing. There under a weeping willow we bake our potatoes buried in cow manure piled under the embers. The manure stinks. The smoke hisses. The idea to bake the potatoes this way came from their eldest brother. Frances and I look at each other, unsure if the advice is a setup. But we are afraid to speak loudly. No one is brave enough to argue with the twins about their eldest brother. Not even their sister. He lives in Germany as an illegal worker in the Munich sewer system and supports the family. A little cow manure stuck to the potato peel, which we took off anyway, was worth giving a stoic family provider his respect.

A decade later Dome would die of some terrible cancer like Mother. Zdeno would become a baker's assistant. After the war started, he supervised the mass executions of Muslim

men that went on late into the night, just like our potato—
night, dark and chilly, high up in the mountains, until there
were no more Muslim men around. Their elder brother would
return from Germany to volunteer for the Croatian army. He
would get killed within a week. That night none of us had any
idea of what was to come as we cursed the cold air and shook
trying to pull the damp clothes away from our skin and force
the shit-baked potatoes down. That night Christians and
Muslims simply sat around a fire together.

* * *

The police show up at my door. The old man Stenek wants
somebody's head in return for the damage, and mine is the
cheapest. Still the officers are a little reluctant to arrest me.
They know who Uncle is. The older one is in his late sixties
and is afraid to be near me. Just get in the backseat, he tells
me. We don't need to cuff you.

The younger one has a long bristling mustache that
reaches past his chin and curls up on either side. He wears the
mustache and the scar under his right eye as decorations.
Proudly. I wonder why he is not forced to shave it off. He
peers at me longer than he should.

You have to come to the station, he says to the opening in
my dress.

Would you let me use your siren? I ask.

We screech as we ride and we scare the cows being loaded
onto a truck and flustered peasants look at us, but we are the
law and they can't say a thing. The older partner grabs his hat
and orders the young man to slow down, slow down

immediately. If he wants to kill himself with the wild girl in the backseat, fine, first let him out.

Gladly, he says.

Where do you want to go? he asks me.

Don't you have to take me to the police station?

Not if you are good.

I let him lie next to me not so I wouldn't get arrested. I let him climb on top of me, between my legs, his uniform smelling like Father's unaired clothes, not because I am afraid of going to jail. I let myself be taken that way, behind the metal screen used to keep a safe distance between the criminals and the law, because the weight of this tall strange man makes me forget about whatever secret Mother's belly hides.

He is rough and uneducated about a woman's body. I think I am his first, which in his mind makes me his wife. I hope I don't throw up all over him, he is so heavy, but he is finished quickly and I can breathe again.

You are so pretty, he tells me, my little princess from the big city, from a big family. I am going to keep you, keep you forever.

. . .

And now he comes every day, and I am weary of him, of the chocolates, lemons, and oranges he brings. His plans. His many plans. His jokes for Grandma. His disdain for my friends. The compliments he pays the keeper, who fancies him. He wants to own a house, build a foundation with his own hands. With trees around it. With some other things I don't want to hear about. The hair on his chest is straight and thin and I miss the way Roderigo's little curls got caught in the fabric of my shirt.

I have a special gift for you, he whispers at the end of the week, and leads me back into the police car. We are weaving up the mountain road to the graveyard.

What are we doing? I ask.

I have never been at the graveyard in the middle of the night, and I am terribly nervous. There is a clearing with a few manicured shrubs. He kneels in front of a round tombstone, takes his gun out, and kisses the marble.

Hello, he says.

The nonsense of talking to someone who is dead and in his grave is more than I can take and I hug him and pull him away.

Samir, please, I want to go.

No. He yanks me down. You will respect my father's grave.

The hard earth scrubs my shins.

He kisses the stone again and fires his gun above the grave, lighting up a picture of a dark-haired man with a stern mustache and eyebrows. She is the one, he screams to the rattled mountain.

. . .

That he was a police officer with only a high-school education would've been enough for the family to disapprove. That he was a grandson of a serf, our own serf to boot, would've been seen as disgrace. They would never have admitted that as a reason, it was against the Party's policy, but while Aunts learned how to play the harmonium and dance the waltz, the serfs spent their time beating the milk fat into butter. Yet nobody said a word. All of the disadvantages could have been accepted and forgotten if they were to be finally rid of me. But when I laughed at his mother, who came to propose a marriage, and said, I am not yet sixteen, not finished with high school, infuriated with rejection, he vandalized my cousin's car, set fire to someone's barn, and got himself arrested. My name ended up on every lip within miles. It was unimaginable.

Now I was a danger to the family. Out with her, let him tame her, however he sees fit. The family pressed Mother hard to sign the release, as I wasn't old enough for legal marriage. She refused. Now the next-door neighbor's phone rang like crazy. Everyone called to say, Let him take her without the papers.

The shame was total and complete. Everybody partook in it. It shook the little town like the Turkish invasion, or at least a rabid raccoon or dog. Except this was far worse: they had a loose woman on their hands.

The good daughters were sent away, safe from the polluted little half-Serbian whore, insatiable between her corrupted juicy legs. They lined up four good Muslim girls in the backseat of a car and headed for the train station, destined for purity. Meanwhile, Uncle drove all day and night without stopping to settle this unpleasant business.

He comes into the room where I am being kept and whispers something into the keeper's ear. She nods and disappears behind Grandmother's door.

First, he slaps me across the face.

You will marry.

No.

He was good enough for you to lie under him, he'll be good enough to feed your filthy wild mouth.

You don't marry any girl you have under you.

The fist is next. There is a warm taste of blood in my mouth and I spit on the floor.

Wipe that.

He pushes me down and rubs my face in my spit. I don't mind. Anything is better than sitting alone in a room unable to speak to anyone. Then he grabs me as hard as he can between my legs and wrings as if he were drying a dishrag.

Listen, you shit, you sick shit, if you do one more thing, one more thing to disgrace this family or to embarrass my poor cousin, I will have you committed to the juvenile delinquent school, the one for the fucking lunatics.

I have heard about what goes on in those places. I have heard about the rapes, the rooms with doors without handles that the male orderlies can go in and out of and do to the girls whatever they want, and the girls have to submit or they are starved. His eyes sparkle. I see he too has heard about the places. They excite him.

I sit back down on the floor, defeated. If I have to marry in order not to go to the reform school, I will. Uncle is triumphant, ready to declare his victory over an enemy deadlier than the Germans.

Mother saves me. There'll be no talk of marriage. She is unflinching: Bring me my daughter back. If it wasn't for

Mother, I would've killed myself. I am sent home four days later on the earliest bus. Frances and Cheery sneak to the train station to wish me good-bye. Frances tells me tearfully, Next time you come back I'll be dead and married. I laugh.

No worries, I say. I'll find you no matter where that baker hides you, even if you are all covered with flour looking like a priceless statue from the Vatican reserved for the pope's holy eyes only.

Your family is right, she blesses herself at the mention of the pope. Why did you soil the Holy Father with your dirty mouth?

My mouth could make him a little less holy, you know, I say. Maybe then he could be a baker.

Cheery knows what I am saying and she gapes at her sister to see the reaction.

Frances snorts, pretending to be angry, and says, I will not be missing you in heaven. I pull her closer to me, and a strange cold bites deep into my chest. I will never see her again, I know.

No, you'll be right next to me in hell, I say. Take care of these kids, I whisper. They know nothing.

My return home is no luxury flight like it was from Cuba. I ride three local buses, jammed with people on their way to different markets. They ask me about my name, my life. I tell them stories. How Fidel liked Mother. They don't know who Fidel is. I tell them he is the hero of the Communist Revolution in a tropical country where colorful pigeons fly outside your windows in dozens. Magical. I wave my arms like the wings. The kind of jungle birds we can see only on TV, on a biology program imported from England called *Survival.* I tell them I had a chocolate-colored Catholic friend whose father was a drummer, and a policeman boyfriend who wanted to marry me.

A woman directly opposite me is knitting a shawl just like the one huddling her shoulders. She has only three fingers but they are deft, and as good as five, she says. She keeps looking at me and then she pulls her stretched-out legs away from mine. Afraid to touch me, I can tell. More afraid my stories might be true.

If you had money to fly to Cuba why are you on this shitty local bus, snaking around the desolate Bosnian mountains? she asks. Why aren't you on a train?

I don't know, I say.

I guess you did something wrong along the way.

. . .

Mother is in the lung hospital. I am told she has a lung virus and that her hair has fallen out because her fever has been really high. When you have a high fever like that, Aunt Dika says, the brain must be protected by rubbing the head with ice, which kills the hair. I come to visit, but she is thick asleep like Uncle when he is drunk. The hospital smells worse than Grandmother's room, and I am mad Mother is here sleeping drunk in this smelly room, and there are no quinces to put under her bed to ease the air. There is only one other woman in the room. She has a lung disease she calls sponging. Her lungs have lost their moisture and are turning into dry sponges, she tells me, as a result of the big war starvation and typhoid fever. The worst thing for the body, she says. Starvation. You better make sure your mother eats something, she warns me. What they are pumping into her veins is poisonous and she must eat.

Mother opens her eyes a little and smiles.

Are you getting better? I ask.

Yes.

A girl told me you had cancer.

Which girl? she asks and closes her eyes.

I don't answer.

Are you hungry? I ask.

She doesn't speak again.

I sit on her bed and wish I was dead or at least drunk with medicine like she is, or with brandy like Uncle is, or even like Frances's pervert uncle is when he is around the girls, and I take a few sips from the rubbing alcohol Dika uses to combat Mother's dangerous temperature. It scorches, and it feels like I'm going to vomit, but warmth spreads through my body.

. . .

It's late September, and school has started. I pack my book bag every morning and go to the bar where I met the soldier after I ran away from Father and the go-carts. I sit outside on the stoop and wait until someone talks to me. Some mornings people go by and nobody says a thing. The bartender opens at ten. Most mornings I get there before he does. He passes me quietly, pulls the gate up, takes the tables out, and sometimes he gives me a Coke and two sugar cubes. I thank him and sit at the table and weave the braids on the tablecloth fringes. Then he asks where my parents are and if I have a home. I tell him I do, and how my father is an ambassador and my mother a professor, and how we have just moved here and I am not starting school until the second semester because we moved here from Cuba and the time over there is upside down because the hot island sits right in the middle of the world and has no seasons, so the school schedule is different.

Big mouth, he says, and he gives me no more Coke. Everybody hates liars.

Then the headmaster calls from school and Dika answers the phone. The girl has not shown up, not once, and doesn't the family know they are liable for what a minor is doing? Who knows what sort of trouble she is getting into during the time she should be getting an education.

Dika hangs up and dials Father. He hangs up and twenty minutes later they are ravaging my drawers. It is the first time I see them together, my war-hero aunt and my educated, white-toothed father side by side, inside my bedroom among the papers, pencils, shirts, rulers.

You haven't been going to school, they say in unison.

Yes, I say.

Why? Father takes over.

Why what?

Sasha! He comes closer.

What? I say again and expect a fist.

You are coming to Greece to live with me, he says.

But I just got back from Bosnia.

I see on Aunt Dika's face I have no choice. The members of the family are united in their decision. I sit on my bed and I wait while they finish examining my things and deciding which of them will be appropriate for my new life. Again.

Part
TWO

6

Athens is the ugliest big city I have ever
seen. Whole families, big families, jumble
together inside square buildings with
seven floors at most. That is the law. The
view of the Acropolis cannot be blocked.
It is a strange law. The center, the famous
monument, is miles and miles away. Way
beyond the eye's reach.

Short stubby women carry tired faces and men look like
they are going nowhere, except when they are riding three
or four together on top of small motorcycles, laughing and
nudging one another while wind flaps their shirtsleeves.
The streets are gray and narrow.

Father is very proud of the area where we are to live.
Glyfada. Right by the sea. It's for the successful, he says. I am
not sure what *successful* means, other than having a marble
floor, a terrace with green plants, for which he had worked so

hard, saved so hard, for years and years, depriving himself, and now we are able to afford to be among the best. We have no furniture yet and we are to sleep on beach mattresses, but we will, next year, he promises, next year, right now the beach mattresses are sufficient. We have the marble floor, for God's sake, he says. Look at those lovely luxurious lines in the marble.

He has a new girlfriend. Dona Stratos. She is not as pretty as my half-brother's mom, but her father owns a tobacco company, which makes her the prettiest. Glyfada is occupied mostly by American soldiers, wealthy Arabs, and a few Greeks. I am to go to school with their children. The school's officials are reluctant to take me without a proper transfer, but Father's new girlfriend makes a handsome contribution for the new gym, and the secretary is all smiles and secretive glances under her caked eyelashes toward Father. The principal shakes his hand firmly.

Welcome to the American Community School. His red skin sags over his collar and I can smell greasy Greek cheese pie on his breath.

Listen, Father tells me, and hands me a wad of colorful bills, go and buy some clothes. And think about the kind of impression you want to make. You are a girl from a house with a marble floor. This could mean a whole new chance to make something of yourself.

I drift among the many stores of our good neighborhood, but I don't like any of the empty, hanging, flat clothes. I follow the highway and the houses get smaller, the marble entrances shrink, the gardens shrivel up, the cars age, and there are more and more people on the street, and each half mile brings more fatigue to the faces and lower prices for the same food.

There is an open market with Greek peasants selling fresh meat and cheese, vegetables sick with heat, cosmetics, even furniture, army trinkets. I bargain over a long, tight plum-color dress with little straps and a pair of metallic-blue high-heel shoes until the woman gives in. I consider telling her I am part Gypsy but she is already back to her cigarette. I change behind a truck and throw away the T-shirt and skirt I was wearing.

There is a flower shop at the corner and I want a flower for my hair like I saw in an Indian sing-along movie. The girl looked like me and a young man fell in love with her and asked to marry her. I go inside and ask if the dried flowers used for the funeral and Christmas arrangements are for sale.

Are you making your own arrangement? the serious gentleman asks me in English.

Yes.

How many flowers do you need?

One.

He is about to yell or throw me out, but he peers up and down and then through my dress slowly, and I see he likes it.

Only one is fine, he says.

It's for my hair, I say.

I haven't shaved my underarms and I can see he likes the way the hair touches the purple cloth. His bald head creases more each time he smiles. He gives me a red flower.

Free for a pretty girl, and he touches my underarm hair with his finger.

I toss the flower into the gutter as soon as I am outside.

The school is quiet when I come in late for the first class. I sit down and don't look at anybody. At first recess I stay close to the classroom and wait to hear what my classmates have to say. I have never seen an American. There is a fat girl who has metal rows of stars across her teeth. She calls them braces and boasts of seeing *E.T.*, which is a movie, twenty times, and how she'd fuck Han Solo, who is not really a person. He is a character from some space movie.

I understand nothing. Not the brown cow feed they eat for breakfast out of soup bowls, not the dry Greek heat. Nothing. At lunch I look for anything to hold on to. And then I see a girl. A beauty, a solace. Narrow feline nose, moon-shaped face. She walks in lazily, sure of herself. She speaks to no one. There's glitter on her eyelids, and I can tell she's gone further than I have, knows more: how to get into trouble without anyone knowing, how not to get pregnant. I revel in her face. Green eyes, black hair, long nose, gapped, sharp teeth.

She sits by herself in the corner. I am mesmerized by the way the chair rubs her bare legs. I carry my lunch tray with nothing on it except a plastic spoon and I sit across from her. The good boys pass us and steal glances. She ignores them.

Not eating? she asks.

Are you kidding? I say.

Where are you from? She studies my face.

A hellhole you never heard about.

You speak funny.

That's how they speak in hellholes.

Nice shoes, she tells me.

You can borrow them anytime.

Len Olivia Fallon. My black-haired Heaven. Her mother is
Greek and her father is American, a union that wouldn't have
been tolerated by the tight community around her mother,
which disapproved of any mixing, but the tall man with gold
California skin and blue eyes had presented himself as a rich
man. Several weeks after the wedding the bride's waist
broadened past the desirable point and the fragile reputation
of the decent couple chipped away. Then the money disappeared, or proved never to have been there, just lies, lies,
and the aunts dismissed the newlyweds as Catholic rabbits,
although Len's father is a Baptist.

What's a Baptist?

A Christian who dips himself in the river water.

So why aren't they called Waterists?

You ask stupid questions like a child, she scorns.

I don't want to be a child. Kids are tedious, she says. She
doesn't like them, and I want her to like me. I want her to take
me to the places she mentions occasionally. The real places. I
have to earn that privilege. I am determined. Whatever she
wants I'll do. I'll wear what she tells me, dance the way she
tells me. I'll be courageous. I love her. When we are in the
movies I lean over and I touch her as much as I can until she
tells me to stop squirming and then I sit properly.

In the beginning I tried to go to classes, I even knew what
floor they were on. I'd walk up the stairs, carry a bag, try to
belong, to understand. Then the school-going shattered.
Each time I opened my notebook, or a textbook, I would see
Mother's face everywhere. Come home, she tells me. Come
home, sweety, she calls for help. Be a good girl, don't eat all

the food on your plate, ladies eat like birds. Be thin, be tender, be lovely.

I want you to try this. Len gives me green leaves packed tight in a plastic bag like the ones for sandwiches. We are in her father's apartment. Her parents are divorced now, and Len's mother's family sent her here after it was discovered she was no longer a virgin.

What is it? I ask.

Don't be an idiot, she barks.

I smoke, and it burns my throat, but I like the way it makes me feel after, all giggly and silly but brave and strong and pretty, and down drops the polluted sway all over my hips and I am tall, tall. Len teaches me how to take a shotgun and it's almost like kissing and I am close to her and I can smell her close to me, and Mother's not in the room, there's nothing wrong right now, and marijuana seems like the best thing in the whole world.

There is a way to feel like this all the time, she says.

How?

Do you feel up for it? She draws near and bites my skin with her razor-sharp teeth, her moon face beaming at me.

Anything, I say.

. . .

Selling drugs was easy then. We were young white girls. It never occurred to me to be afraid of ending up in handcuffs. Or at least it never occurred to me that I could not get myself out of trouble any way I had to. I walked around smiling with bags stashed inside my bra or between my legs. I was drunk and losing my mind, and had no idea. I strolled around Piraeus, the largest drug-receiving port in the Mediterranean, with a smile on my face. The police pulled their car over next to me on the street once, asked what I was doing there. I told them I was visiting a friend. They offered to give me a lift. The Greek police cars smelled different than Bosnian ones. We drove around in a circle until I told them I forgot where my friend lived, and they dropped me off back where they had picked me up, on the big street in the middle of the port bursting with intoxicating goods from faraway places.

Father is happy I no longer ask for any money and never eat at the house. He doesn't ask me where I go. Sometimes I catch him shaving in the morning and I pretend to sneak in, and he pretends not to hear I just got home, and we go on pretending and ignoring each other.

Len and I go to the beach, sit in the sun, let the silly Greek men buy us wine and beer and whiskey and shells and lobster, and when we are alone with them, I do whatever Len does, whatever she wants to do. We have our funny names for it, sitting on the box, hiding in the box, bursting the box, and I give her all the money, let her call all the shots, and when she smiles I can see Mother smile and be proud of me, and I am finally happy.

7

Everything comes to a sudden change
here in winter. The sun-people have
forgotten all about winter and they are
aghast at the way the cold wind bites. They
huddle together as they are waiting for the
buses, which are late as if the weather
were still hot and good, and easy, and they
complain how the country has gone to hell
with a little bit of northern wind on its
back and they look strangely at my naked
limbs and bare feet that love the cool air.

Michaly is the dealer. He is Len's friend and thinks I am
twenty. You are dazzling, he tells me whenever I see him, and
he sits sideways so he can see between my legs or inside my
shirt.

He gives us a block of hash to deliver to a Burmese diplomat across town. Len says we should pinch some of it for

ourselves first. We have several hours to kill and Len's hungry, she says. She doesn't want to eat the stupid Greek food, only American. I offer to cook American spaghetti.

What's American spaghetti? she asks.

You add ketchup and feta.

Father is away. Away with his rich girlfriend who loves him. And he loves her. He rushes out the door when she honks the horn on her expensive German car, and never says when or if he'll be back.

The pot lid bounces over the boiling water and I shake to the rhythm of a song playing on the radio. Len is trying to shave a piece of hash for us without leaving a mark. Burmese or not, the diplomat can't be that stupid. The front door opens and Father enters. He looks at me with the same disinterest he always does. Panicked, I take the block of hash and I throw it in the bubbling ketchup. Len pales. I push as hard as I can on the block with a spatula until it starts to melt.

Then Father sees Len. His eyes measure her body slowly, a glint of interest budding. I recognize the look. An awe that alters the face of a man, reserved for special girls like Len and Mother, slender beauties with modest lines, nothing springing out of the front of their bodies, nothing in the back, nothing to provoke a man, to disturb him and cause him to bark like they do when I go by. Before such temperance in shape they gape quietly with wonder as Father does now. And like with Mother, men want to do things to please her, for her, not to her.

Are you Sasha's friend from school? he asks.

Yes.

Would you like some fresh lemonade?

Thanks.

I am fuming. He talks to me only to tell me not to eat so much pita, how I will regret it later when I am too plump and it's too late. He pulls his chair very close to Len's. Since I refuse to dye my hair blond, he keeps as far away from me as he can. He shields himself in the store, so nobody thinks I'm his. When we are at the beach, he inches away, pretending to grab pebbles with his toes. I know he is nothing like the proud fathers who sit close to their pretty daughters, claiming them, scaring away other men, all the bad men with evil designs.

I am not regal. I am not blond. I remind him of his dark Gypsy ancestors, of his father's beatings, things he wants to forget. The tears inside me simmer, suffocate, and the birds chirping outside the window mock me: Your father doesn't care, doesn't care for a good-for-nothing girl.

Do you want some pasta, Daddy? I ask.

He is too wrapped up in Len's white skin to realize I just called him Daddy, which should have been alarming enough. Len stabs me with a what-is-the-matter-with-you look, but I ignore her and slam the plate in front of him and pour the sauce until it leaks over the edge and he scoffs, Why do you always have to make a mess?

Father eats. Len watches.

This is good, he says. Did you give her the recipe? he asks Len.

She doesn't answer.

Are you all Greek? He continues to appraise Len's long arms and legs, green eyes, signs of good white breeding.

Not completely. My father's family is from California, but Ireland before that.

Ah, the lovely Celts, he says.

Do you want some more? I interrupt.

No. He's starting to slur. We should do something fun. Let's play a game. He leans over and touches Len's pale arm. Would you like to play a game? he asks.

Sure.

How's Monopoly?

I mumble, Fine, and he looks at me as if he had forgotten I was there.

I am winning. Father is too stoned and Len too unfocused. He's screaming, Bitch, take my fucking money. *Ade ke gamisou. Sta arhidia.* Cursing in Greek. I have never heard Father curse in any language before. He insists that public behavior is sacred and must be cherished, but Michaly's dope has cracked his resolve. Len laughs each time he touches her, and I want him to keel over and die, but I have seen *Midnight Express,* and something tells me I wouldn't enjoy Greek prisons if I was doing life for killing my father with enough hash to tranquilize all of Burma.

An hour later, he's passed out. I check him for breath.

Is he all right? Len asks.

He's breathing.

You don't like him much.

Fuck him.

Tough little bitch, you are, she tells me.

We better wash everything, she says, and we pile pots and pans in the sink.

I say nothing.

What are we going to tell Michaly? she asks.

I don't care.

You'll care when he comes after us.

I'll take the blame, don't worry.

Like I said. Tough little bitch.

I empty Father's wallet and throw the worn-out leather over the neighbor's fence.

Here, take this. I give her the money. That'll do.

Len is gone and the apartment is quiet. I turn all the lights off. Father is sprawled on the couch, his lips lightly parted, the night air pouring though the open window. I take a beer out of the refrigerator and sit by his feet. He opens his eyes, but he has no idea I am close.

I had a nice day at school, I whisper into the darkness. The teacher said I am a really good writer, and that I will go places if I work hard.

There is no answer. I touch his fingers. They are hairy and thick. He lets out a sigh and adjusts a little. I sip my beer and rub his head. His hair is wiry and strong like mine.

I want to leave this place, Dad, I say and touch the bump on his nose. Leave you too, Dad. You too.

There are sounds and commotion at the next-door neighbor's. The heat is finally on, and the kids are running around glad to be rid of their sweaters, jeering at the radiators, while their mother is warning, Don't get too close to the leaking steam, especially not with bare feet. You'll slip, break your necks, and get burned. I hear laughter. I take another sip from the beer bottle and whisper, I love you, Dad, to the wall.

. . .

The money in Father's wallet doesn't satisfy Michaly. He expects a favor. I have to deliver a suitcase. He looks at me like I'd better not fuck up this one. I don't. I deliver a smelly suitcase to the address, and I am disappointed at the neatness of the house. A tall woman smiles, takes the suitcase, and closes the door.

A week before Christmas Father announces he is going away with his Dona, he insists on calling her his now, and if I want a big New Year's celebration I should go home to Yugoslavia. Len has promised to introduce me to the American GIs. The suitcase delivery has finally earned me an introduction.

I have things to do for school, I say.

Father suspects I am lying but has no interest or energy to investigate. His shirts are back from the dry cleaners' and his pants and jacket are new. He is rushing to see his Dona, his heiress, his love, who's been so generous during the season of giving, and who has a real wood-burning fireplace, and lives on the top, most fashionable floor of a famous building in the most expensive part of town, and could do a lot for Father's business. After all, I should know how unwelcoming Greeks are to foreigners, how untrusting.

. . .

There is really no GI colony. Nobody is fenced in here like in the other bases in other countries, Len says. The soldiers live among the Greeks. The landlords are reluctant to rent to the Americans. The nationalists are calling it treason. They are descendents of Plato, the ancients. But American dollars stretch a long way, much longer than drachmas. The landlords give in to temptation, and the apartments are listed on base. The blacks are even more of a problem. Greeks hate to see Americans darker than the Turks or Gypsies with more money than they have.

Here we are, Len says as we pull into the wide driveway. When I introduce you, act smart, Len says.

I will.

The apartment is Cole's. He is short and it takes me a while to understand what he is saying. I am a country boy, he says, from Paducah, western Kentucky, famous for lawn-mower races. He was the first local black man to compete. Almost won too, but, afraid of all the rednecks, he slowed down right before the end. Not until he went to a competition in Mississippi did he allow himself the real victory.

I thought Mississippi is a river, I say. How can you drive over a river? They all laugh, You really are a foreigner, despite that smooth Yankee accent. She just has a way with languages, Len says. She's good with Greek too, but she has no clue, and they all laugh. I wonder if they would let me try the brown powder that is on the table.

Cole? I ask. What kind of a name is that?

Cool. Like Cole Porter.

Who's that? I ask.

This girl, they say. That's some foreign shit for you.

Maybe foreign, but not a shit, I say, and they laugh even louder.

There is a big stereo system with a TV and a couch in the middle of the room facing the TV. The Lakers game is on. They tell me it's a basketball team from L.A. I am surprised the game would be on in the middle of the day, but they tell me it's the tape from the old finals. I love basketball, I say.

I like KC the best. He is tall and quiet and sits in a smart way and scopes the room. He is from New York.

I'm going to move there, I say.

You should. You've got an air about you, baby.

What air? I ask.

Like you don't give a damn.

I know who Clark Gable is, I say. He didn't gave a damn, either.

And they all laugh again, The girl is killing me, killing me, man.

Len puts the shot glasses, lemon, and salt on the table. Tequila warms my body. The room stretches a little. KC puts the movie in. *The Warriors.* A movie about New York gangs.

I was in one of them, he says. The police arrested me, and threw me in the army.

I got thrown in the backseat by the cops, I tell him. Asked to take my clothes off.

Sorry, he says. But look at you now. Tough like Swan's girlfriend from the Bronx. Look at them, he points at a couple on TV. On their way to Coney Island.

How far is Coney Island?

Far away for these guys.

Come on, man, Cole says. Cut it out with the movie. Let's do a line.

KC asks me if I've done this before, and I look at the TV, at the mass of gang members, Cyrus's soldiers standing close together looking at the ocean. They belong. I look at the brown pile. It offers a place among these people. Sure, I've done it before, I say. I am glad tequila is making me dull, because the brown stuff burns my nose.

KC asks me to dance. It's different than in Cuba. The music is slow and heavy and we are closer, rubbing, and I ask him, What kind of music is this? and he says, R&B. I want to say, Like Rhett Butler, and make everyone laugh and like me, but a strange calm spreads over me, a kind of calm I never knew before. A woman cries beautifully on the record, and he tells me it's Billie, and I say, I would name my daughter Billie, and he whispers, No, not Billie, she was a sad lady. There, there, you're a natural, look at you, made to drive men crazy for a while and leave them after. Glad to come into your path while you still don't know it, little girl.

We fall into the gentle clop of drunken conversation.

Where is your mom? he asks and fixes my hair.

Away.

Yeah? And you are all by yourself?

Uh-huh.

How old are you?

Twenty.

Sure?

Sure. How about you?

Forty-one.

How long have you been a soldier?

Almost sixteen years.

Long time.

How long have you been this pretty?

I smile and close my eyes.

He kisses and kisses and mumbles Sweet baby to my neck and my face and Ah, such lovely breasts, and we are on the

bed and his warmth is pressed against me, and each time I
move or roll over he is there waiting, his head in my lap and
the music around us, between us, and the streetlight seeping
gray through the curtain and the car engines overpowering
the music and then disappearing and his voice calling me
Beautiful, beautiful and the calm, heavy calm carried by the
brown powder eases the craving that dashes between my legs
in the presence of men, and I feel a long, precious nothing.

. . .

The morning sun is reddening my cheek and I am still slug-
gish and murky, and Cole knocks hard on the door: Let's go,
man, we have PT in twenty minutes. Take the number or have
Glyfada Len bring her around later.

Hey, fucker, don't call me that, Len screams, and I know
she is pissed, pissed about the name that clings to her.
Glyfada Len. I've heard about it in school. Black GIs from all
over the world about to be stationed in Greece, which they call
an eighteen-month vacation, are unofficially briefed about
Glyfada Len, a young beauty willing to party and everything
else. Just throw a couple of bucks at her for a good time. The
gullible country boys are warned not to get attached 'cause
Glyfada Len is everybody's girl.

KC whispers, It's morning, sweet baby, into the patch of
hair across my face, and tells me, I'll see you at Club 57
tonight. I don't know where the club is but I say sure. They
leave in a hurry. Len and I stay behind. The good girls'll clean
up, she promises. As soon as the door is closed she tears up
Cole's drawers looking for the picture of his girlfriend. We

find a wedding picture, Cole in a ruffled light-blue shirt next to a girl in a white dress.

Fucker's married! Len throws the picture away, and I pick it up carefully and put it back.

I don't care if he finds out, she says.

Do you care he's married? I ask.

Do you care KC has a wife?

Should I?

No. Just don't fall for him. They all leave after their term, leave the white pussy behind and return to their lives in the States. But who gives a shit. This is our time. We are their ladies now, she laughs, and we reopen the last bottle of tequila and watch *The Warriors* again.

   . . .

Nobody cares how old you are when you go to a club here, as long as you pay the cover: one hundred drachmas, which is almost a dollar. It's a little steep, Len says, but if we are smart, we don't have to pay for drinks. Once you get a steady guy to buy your drinks the owner tells the bouncers to let you in for free. Until then pay a hundred, and sit and wait for the guys.

It's Friday, and the club is full of Africans who bring the brown powder I now know is heroin. Len tells me, Ride it easy. The Africans keep it stuffed inside wooden matchboxes and they exchange it with GIs for hair products and cash.

There is a fresh newcomer—Sha from Paterson, New Jersey, and one would think from his stories Paterson is the best place in the world. Real tough gangs and lots of women, he says. Sha's already been picked up by Despina, who is

lovely and forty and rarely takes a new guy. I wait for them to
be broken down, softened by the dry hot weather, she tells
Len, but this one is special. I stand behind and watch. They
are wearing matching red T-shirts. His says "I love Despina";
hers, "I love Sha." She works at the Massage Palace. When she
hears I am Len's friend and may be looking for a job, she tells
me there is a hookup at the massage parlor where she works
and she can get me in no problem. There's good money,
better than waiting tables or cleaning, but you have to be
ready to give the "full-release" massages. You can do it with
gloves on if it grosses you out. Extra tip if you can do it with
your mouth. I don't understand what she means. She laughs
and explains.

I am nauseous. The table by the dance floor is empty.
There is never a sign on it, but people know not to go near it.
It's reserved for the white women who come to the club on
the weekends. They are English and Scottish with nanny
jobs. They don't come out every night. The guys date them
seriously, pay their rent, buy them clothes, drive them to
work. The local Greek girls, a few girls from Sri Lanka, which
is near India and even hotter, Len tells me, and the rest of the
brown, olive, and black girls who come to the club all the
time, every night, have to take the tables in the back.

It's best to speak English. The girls who speak English
well are the most respected. There are a few Brazilian girls
who are really pretty and young and fun, but they don't speak
English and even if the guys really like them, they never
become girlfriends with house keys, car keys, birthday
presents, and sweet words. Like us, they come and sit and wait
to be asked. Even if they are prettier, much prettier, than the

pink bitches, Len says, and can shake their asses better than some of the American girls. The men are all black. There isn't a single white man here, although everybody says it's different in the States. There you can see white men everywhere.

Len points to a Greek couple, says, Look at that sicko, he likes to watch. She wears a see-through dress to make sure she scores with someone. The husband hides inside a closet. They pretend he is not home, put up this whole act. She's gotten fat and old, and now they can only catch the strung-out Africans. None of the GIs pick her up anymore. He's been trying to get her on some of Michaly's dope to make her skinny. I am afraid to look at her at first, but I do slowly and she smiles at me when she catches me staring. I wish I knew her name so I could say hello.

KC enters and he's wearing a suit. Everybody can tell it's new. He walks directly toward me, seeming a little nervous. Asks me if I want a drink and would I sit at the front table where we can talk.

Lucky, Len mumbles. I sit up proudly and say, Rum and Coke, which is Len's favorite. The drink is tasty and cold. I say thank you and smile, and Len scoffs, The little wench, learning so quickly.

How old are you? he asks again.

Twenty, I told you.

If I believed you, I wouldn't have asked again.

Twenty, I say.

Are you in junior high or in high school?

Even if I'm younger than you think, I'm not stupid enough to fall for your trick question.

You are a bad girl. He smiles. And jailbait.

Do you care how old I am?

I don't know, sweet baby, just don't know. You can get me in a lot of trouble.

'Cause you're married?

And that's just the beginning.

The ice clinks against my teeth. I swallow and think about ways to keep him. He can't leave. He must stay. He is nice to me. And strong. Stronger than Father. I am proud to be sitting next to this strong man at the front table drinking a drink. Why can't I be at least eighteen, big enough to be a girlfriend, in the front seat of an imported car? And I remember Gordana and Uncle and I press my forehead against his and say, Please, please stay, I'll be good. I'll be so good, you're gonna want to be with me all the time. You're gonna want to leave your wife and your kid and do everything for the little nobody jailbait from nowhere.

You're something, he says.

No, I am not, I say, but I'll be anything you want me to be.

. . .

There are parties. The Thursday, the Friday, the Saturday, the no-reason parties. There is nothing to do during the dreary Greek winter with no tourists. The locals are bored and more racist than in summer when there are plenty of white girls, more girls than guys even. But the blondes have returned to their cold countries and the good Greek girls are at home, and the Greek men are angry at the Americans and their American money, so they want to fight. KC says the little boys are not worth the trouble and Let's go, baby, let's do some lines in the car. Who's having a party tonight?

So we sit in the car and nod, and relax and watch the planes land and take off between the blue and red lights, and we kiss and talk, do some more lines, and nod out again. People pass the car and look at us, at me, at him, and they hurry their steps.

Are you going to school? he asks.

No.

Why?

I just don't.

He nods. I nod.

What kind of a school is it?

Are you talking about school again? I come back from my nod.

No, still.

We are parked in front of a house. The lights go on inside. The sound of the door screeching scrapes my ears and a man sticks his head out.

Fyge, he yells.

They want us to leave? KC asks.

I say nothing and crinkle the paper in my pocket. I ran into two Australian girls I know from the beach. Joanna and Gaylia. We Aussies are like the English, they kid, but we tan better. They have a huge apartment on the water. Once a month they visit the United Arab Emirates and return carrying bags of gowns, jewelry, and cash rich sheiks gave them as presents. You should come, Gaylia says. You may have some trouble with those dark eyes and hair, but that body! The Arabs would kill for that body. Call this number, don't be silly, you don't have to do anything you don't want to. The number is on the paper.

What time is school? KC asks.

It's in the morning, I say.

. . .

News travels fast among soldiers: KC's lost it for his teenage white girl. The wife's gone home for an Easter visit and now she threatens not to come back. No wonder. He's even brought the girl to the apartment where he lives with his wife and baby K. The girl is poor, from some Red country.

KC has the same furniture as everyone else's. The discount furniture store, he says. Same in baby K's room except smaller.

Don't you feel guilty for cheating on your wife? I ask.

That's a funny question coming from you.

Why?

Because I'm cheating with you.

But I'm not cheating.

You're a strange girl.

Later in bed he tells me she was pregnant when he married her and how he is not really sure if they love each other, if they ever loved each other. My parents loved each other for a moment, I say. He watches my body as I speak. I am naked. He touches me. And now Mother has cancer, I say. I am not sure he is listening.

Love is complicated between men and women, he says into my ear. You are young and you don't know yet.

Is it always sad? I ask.

Yes.

Is it different between men? I ask.

Between soldiers it is. I love the soldiers more than anything other than baby K, who is life itself.

My father loves my little half brother like that, I say.

What about you?

Oh, he doesn't even like me. He likes his marble floor.

I like you, baby, he tells me.

You don't have to be my father.

Who are you? he says and pulls me closer.

A strange girl, I say.

Sleep, he whispers. Sleep.

* * *

The first morning we don't have to hide is beautiful. Hot. The bugs shatter their brittle wings against the warm window glass. Beach, beach, KC whispers. Let me take you to the beach so that every pervert can envy me. We pack as if we were a real couple, towels in the same bag. He calls my tanning lotion "paying to be blacker."

I take the bundle of money from my pocket and give it to him.

What's this? he asks.

I've been selling dope.

So?

I thought . . .

Keep it.

I drop my head down and look outside the window. He

slows the car down a little. That money is yours, he says. I don't want it. I like you anyway.

I squeeze the money in my hands and wish I could call him Mom. He is the nicest person I know, and I wish I were his daughter.

. . .

KC doesn't know how to swim. I say, Relax, sweet baby, I'll teach you how. I help him float on his back with his legs wrapped around me. People are watching and I tell everybody he can't swim. They laugh and clap when he manages on his own for a second. Then I show him how to swim underwater, and he is swimming toward me like the babies at home, in the kind Adriatic, the way Momma taught me how to swim before I was three years old, and took a picture of me and put it in the album for the whole world to see. Afraid of salt, he keeps his eyes closed, and when he runs into my belly he stands up scared. I hold his face in my hands and kiss his salty lips and tell him, I love you.

Later I show him how to crack a lobster and eat it properly and not make a mess. He wants a bib, but I frown on it. There are no bibs here after you turn five. He says, Fuck this crafty eating country, we still own it, and if it wasn't for us, they'd all be speaking Turkish.

Neither of us can sleep that night. I think of Mother, of her body that is bowing to cancer. I wonder if she ever had a lover. She once told me about a friend who had been seen getting in a car with a younger man. The friend was married. Her husband was rich and away. The younger man was a poet.

He wrote sad poems to Mother's friend and they both cried. The husband returned and it was the end of it. Nobody knew what became of the poet.

The curtain is caught in the window and KC gets up to fix it. He stands by the window. He speaks without turning around.

Some of my friends on base are in trouble.

What kind of trouble? I ask.

Their urine tested positive.

Positive?

Yes, for dope.

Is that so bad?

When you are a GI it's pretty serious.

What about you?

We'll see.

Is there anything I can do?

I know there is nothing I can do, I don't even understand him, or what is going on.

You can sit real close to me and breathe into my face and be my sweet baby, he whispers.

I love you, I say.

*   *   *

There is no light in the house a day and a half later when I return. Just a small burning dot tracing in the air on the terrace. It can't be Father. Father doesn't smoke.

What was that? he asks.

What was what?

I either am mistaken, or there was no driver in that car.

There was.

What have you been doing? he asks.

I was at a friend's.

Look on the kitchen table. He takes a drag and coughs.

There is a piece of paper on the kitchen table informing him I haven't been to school in more than a month. I can feel the swell of a big fight. I have wasted all that hard-earned money for tuition.

What was that you fed me months ago that made me so sick?

I don't know.

Oh, yes, you do, and he flings the cigarette over to the street. What are you going to become? A streetwalker?

Don't be paranoid, I say.

He stands up and walks over to the front door. He opens it.

Get out of my house, he says. And don't come back.

Get out, he repeats, and walks into the kitchen, opens the refrigerator, and opens a can of Sprite. Just go!

I wish he had beat me. Pulled my hair, so I could have cried, or tried to fight back, or tumbled and bled on his precious marble. Anything would have been better than just opening the door. I pack only a few shirts. The dope is too strong to be dragging a heavy load around. I take a picture frame with Mother's photo. That's where I hide my dope. Father is still in the kitchen and doesn't say anything when I walk out.

I drag my half-empty suitcase toward the beach. Cars pass me. There would be no more school, trying not to nod off while Mrs. Donaldson explains things I never understand.

Good, I think, and snort two long lines as the night erases the sea, except for the white foam busting from the tops of the waves.

.   .   .

Len says, Let's try Monica and Emmanuelle. You can't stay with me, my father would be all over you. Especially drunk. Monica and Emmanuelle are Brazilian and generous and people always crash there. Len's right. They are all hugs and supportive glances. Take the floor, sweets. Here is a pillow. Cover yourself with a jacket. We are short on blankets, but you are good with the cold. It must be nothing for those big Viking limbs.

I'm a Slav, not a Viking.

Viking, Slav, it's all big, right?

Right.

So you won't be cold.

I think they are much older than they say they are. Len says they're lying to make themselves younger. Nobody wants an old bag around here. Only Despina gets away with it, but she is exquisite.

We were political, Emmanuelle says. My passport is wrong. I changed the birth year to make myself older. The government keeps the children in the country.

Really? I ask.

It's a good trick, she says and smiles.

Emmanuelle smiles all the time, which guys like the most, but Monica has straight hair. Straight hair is a coveted asset among the descendants of the kinky-haired African slaves. Makes us look more white, she says. The apartment is small and filthy. There is a window but it overlooks a wall. The landlady is a Greek woman. She spews, Hookers, hookers, when we pass by. She hikes up the rent every other month but never asks the girls to move.

Emmanuelle and Monica call the guys their boyfriends. On weekends guys spend all day at the apartment, eat rice and beans, spend time alone with the girls in their bedrooms. After, we all sit in the front room and listen to the radio and dance. There is no TV. Sometimes guys bring hair-food and straightening products. I never see any cash. The girls see only one guy at a time. It seems a fair exchange to me. My job is to wash out their bras and the underwear they call G-strings, air their dresses, pants, and shirts from smoke, and do the dishes. They call me *Formosa*, the beauty, and promise to take me to Rio some day.

Monica's new boyfriend, Larry, is white. From Jacksonville, Florida, which is in the northern part of Florida but is more Confederate than the south of Florida, he says, because of all the Jews. Ever since Monica met Larry she's been acting like a snob. She bought a hat at the market, a wide-rimmed ugly straw thing, ties a scarf around it, and wears it every day he comes around.

Emmanuelle and I hate Larry. He acts like he is *muito bonito*, Emmanuelle says, always talking about Florida. Stupid Florida. If it's so good in Florida, why are you in Greece? she asks him.

'Cause I like you girls. All of you, and I'm going to be so bored when I go home.

Monica's been hoping for months he'd sponsor her visa to go to the States and his talking about leaving hurts her. He unzips her shirt and puts his hands on her breasts.

I am going to miss these the most, he says.

I spit in his eggs and revel in the joy on Emmanuelle's face as he takes his first bite. Yes, Senhor Larry, I say, you'll miss us *muito*.

. . .

All the girls are after the new dj. Even the navy girls, who are in for the weekend. Despina is pissed because Sha is dancing with one of them, young and full of brand-new club moves.

The local pussy was good enough for him Tuesday but there is something wrong with it on Friday? She is livid.

The navy girls are full of their own dollars and American tricks and know how to say, We don't need no water, let the motherfucker burn, along with the music. It doesn't sound silly like when Greeks try to imitate it.

The floor shakes and I think the dancing is so good we are moving the building, but then the military police storm the place. The music stops. The tallest MP leaps over the several steps in front of the dj's booth, pushing away the line of girls. What the fuck? rumbles through the party air.

The MP grabs the microphone and says, Is this thing on? He meant to ask only the dj, but the thing is on and we all hear him, and the whole room snickers at his clumsiness.

Men and women, he says in a grave and responsible voice that reminds me of Aunt Dika, we have a situation. A bomb exploded at the bar next door. Four of our men are injured. I am here to ask you to get back on base and report to your senior officers for the head count.

The air changes, and panic spreads.

We don't know if there are more elements circling around, the MP continues. Move it, move it. The orders are clear.

A river of people trickles toward the narrow door.

Let's wait for the crowd to clear out, KC says.

Outside there are ambulances and screaming and lots of people. We inch through to the corner to Bobbies, the bar that exploded. The wounded Greeks are carried into Greek ambulances, the Americans into their own. A Greek woman with bloodstained arms screams, *Fyge apo tin hora mas!*

What's she saying? KC asks.

Get out of our country, I translate.

Stupid assholes. If we left, the Turks'd be here in a second.

What's the difference who occupies your country? I ask.

Big one, he says.

Then he stops and looks at me funny. We bring freedom, he says.

Like that? I point at the segregated ambulances. Like at Club 57, no mixing.

His eyes are probing.

When did you grow up? he asks.

. . .

Downtown is off-limits. I don't see KC for three days. I go to Len's house for news. She tells me everyone is staying on base and she is not sure what's going to happen. Papandreou, the Greek president, promises a quick solution to the problem. There was a mandatory urine test for everyone on base. Seems something's up with KC's. His test came back loaded, and this is not the first time, so he might be up shit creek, which is very bad. There's a rumor that Cole made a deal for himself by naming KC as a dealer. He could be locked up at Leavenworth, for who knows how long. And after? A lousy Bronx job, and a shit future for the sweet baby K.

KC's home after another day, unkempt and tired.

Hi baby, he smiles when I show up. Pull up a chair.

Michaly sent over consolation dope. Len drops a bag on the table.

Fuck it, KC says and snorts five huge lines. There'll be no more testing for me. I'm finished anyway. Len signals to me like I should do something.

Careful, KC, I tell him. He makes a line for me.

Try this. He gives me the straw. It's awesome.

*   *   *

I should have taken care of him that day. The way he took care of me before. As if I were his child. I should have loved him that much that day. I shouldn't have done a line. I should have soothed, kissed him. Taken him to bed, taken him inside of me, made him forget. But I hadn't slept in days and I missed him. And I missed being high. So I gave in and took the straw. I still remember how good the dope was. He was right as always. It was awesome. I closed my eyes for a moment.

It's dark when I wake up alone on the floor in baby K's bedroom. I can't hear anybody in the front of the house. My mouth is crusted with snot. Baby toys hang upside down, glued to the ceiling. A rabbit, a moose, an angel, and a turtle.

Out in the front room, KC's head is leaning against the table with a small trickle of vomit on one side of his face. His eyes are slightly open. He looks like he's sleeping, but I know he is not. There's more vomit on a bag of diapers sitting on the table. I take it off the table and put it down on the floor. KC hates a mess. Once in a movie I saw a man check another man for a pulse, so I do the same. I think I feel something, but I know I have imagined it. I close his eyes and leave.

. . .

At the beach the sun is warm and the water is clear. No waves at all. Summer has returned and drawn out the happy tourist girls and the handsome Greek men. Emmanuelle finds me. She sits close, doesn't make any jokes. She acts her real age. Len and Michaly are held for questioning, she says, and Len said something about me being a Russian spy who infiltrated U.S. soldiers, and how I had something to do with the people who bombed Bobbies. She also said I was there when KC died and they were thinking about waiting to rule out homicide until they spoke to me. The police knocked at Monica and Emmanuelle's twice already looking for the "minor" who stayed on their floor. They were cute too, and Monica offered them some eggs.

I know you are not a spy, Emmanuelle says, but we can't afford to be dealing with the Greek *Astynomia*.

I understand. Once I saw the Greek police beat students with wooden sticks. Father and I were having lunch. The restaurant manager pulled the gates down and very politely told his customers to please enjoy their meal. The unpleas-antries would soon be over.

Trapped, the students clung to the gate. The Greek police caught up. Their nightsticks were shiny and moved through the air like a conductor's stick. They kept perfect time with one another as they beat their captives. It was as impressive as it was disgusting. Father never said to turn away. I watched, curious, until they bled so hard I could not tell who was who.

I was not about to be questioned.

You will go away. Understand? Emmanuelle says.

I will. Right away.

Got any money?

No.

Larry left and took all of Monica's jewelry.

Figures.

Motherfucker.

She'll be fine, I say.

You'll be fine too.

I love you, I tell her before I leave.

I know. You my sister, my *Formosa*.

I have only thirty drachmas. French fries cost seventy. I haven't eaten since the previous morning. I try Father's but the key won't go into the lock. Smart move on his part really, but I manage to snake up the vine and over the fence and soon I am swallowing olives. I wonder why there is no bread and see a lot of dust on the counter and I realize he is no longer in Greece. He hadn't only kicked me out—he had left me.

However, he didn't disconnect the phone. It takes years to get a phone in Greece. I am grateful for the inefficiency as I dial Dika's number. There's a husky hello.

Dida, I say. I haven't called her that in a long time.

My God, where are you? she yells in a dry voice and coughs. I hear the crinkling of plastic paper as she reaches for her cigarettes. We've been sick with worry. Your father told us you were missing.

I'm not. He kicked me out.

He told us you were with another black man and then you disappeared.

You know him. He's a liar.

She is quiet, thinking. He may be a liar, but I am not much better ranked.

You should come home, she says.

How?

I'll get you a ticket for this afternoon. Just get yourself to the airport.

Okay.

Alexandra? she says. She never calls me that.

Yes?

Aren't you going to ask about your mother?

How is she?

Terrible.

. . .

I have my passport in my pocket with the number of KC's friend in New York, Spivey, scribbled on the back of it. I walk straight to the airport, which takes me two hours. The woman at the Yugoslavian airline counter already has my name. She gives me ten dollars, which I spend on two orders of French toast I don't eat and a beer I drain immediately.

The passengers are loading at the terminal. It seems everyone stops and looks at how dirty I am. My toenails are chipped and uneven. There's a bruise on my left ankle. I don't know where it came from. The pretty straps on my shoes make my filthy skin look even worse. My hair and my clothes are just as bad. No wonder Father left. Who wouldn't?

I step out of the way and let the good people by. I don't really belong here among this niceness, kindness, responsibility. Mother is dying or she is dead, and KC is dead already, and I am not yet sixteen, and I am not sure what I'm supposed to do, so I back off from the entrance and let more good people on until there is no one else waiting to get on the plane, and a nice stewardess, all smiles and sweet stewardess smells, wraps her uniformed arm around me and ushers me. Come on, darling, come on, it's time to fly home.

8

All I really know of the cousin who greets
me at the airport is that he wants to
become an actor. Damian. "Silky"
Damian. He threatens to take his clothes
off onstage for the whole world to see his
thing. His mother wants him to be
respectable, but she is still blamed for
everything. His strangeness. He spends
hours locked in the bathroom. His slow-
ness. The way he chews his food, on one
side of the mouth, then the other, like an
old cat.

Our family breeds strength and bravery, Aunt Dika says.
That weepy woman who married into our family shouldn't
have had sons. What can you expect from someone born
across the Danube? A woman from far up north, with a slow,
lazy accent and a tendency to eat too much cake. Nothing good

comes out of stuffing your mouth with sugar, just mushy entrails. The northern corpses rot quicker than the Bosnian highlanders' because they are all spoiled on the inside years before they're dead.

We call him Silky for always being sick. Growing up, he was not allowed to run. He cried once, in front of everybody. We had a family competition that day to see which of the kids would stay in the freezing water the longest. His bottom lip shook after I fearlessly flung myself off the edge and broke all the records. Everyone in the family laughed. Except for his mother. She tried hugging him until her husband, another engineer Uncle, yelled, Leave him, he is not made out of silk.

He is different today. Quiet as always but he looks at me with those big eyes, sissy eyes, like he's sorry. We line up for the bus. It's hot, too hot. All the men look at my tanned skin. They remind me of Larry. I hope whoever is home making their dinner spits in their dishes tonight.

Silky minds that they are looking at me, tries to get in between me and the crowd to intercept the glances.

Do you want to put on my sweater? he asks.

It's hot.

Still.

It won't stop them, I say.

What?

The guys. Sweaters don't stop them.

He looks at me for a long time.

Sorry, he says.

Mother is alone in her hospital room, surrounded by tidy beds with tight bedcovers. The doctors told her she has a rare form of consumption and they are keeping other patients separate. She has shrunk and looks tiny and weak, but there is a restraint across her waist.

Why is she strapped? I ask the young doctor who followed me in. He has a kind face and deep eyes and labors to sound grown up.

Let me explain, he starts. She was restless at night and she tore the curtain rod off the wall. It's better for her this way.

She weighs less than a hundred pounds, I say.

Pain is powerful.

He retreats, expecting a scene, that I will scream and cry. He's been trained to handle the routine of grief.

I can imagine, I say, to spare the young doctor.

He touches my arm gratefully, says, She is not feeling anything.

Can I have some of that?

We all need it sometimes. He smiles. But it wouldn't do you any good. You should go home and be with your family. It won't be long now.

I'll sit with her awhile.

Go home.

Mother has dry scabs on her skull. I don't believe the curtain story, so I untie her. She is burning, her eyes drowning in terror. The whites around her pupils are yellow.

I'm scared, she says to the room.

Don't be, I whisper.

I'm afraid for you.

She is not hallucinating, I realize.

I kiss her and keep my lips on her dry cheek until I am burning with her. Her skin's parched as if she were dead already.

I'm a big girl, I say.

You're a baby.

I lean over, close to her ear. Nobody else knows that, I say. Only me and you.

I take the bottle of brandy from my pocket and lie down next to her. It sounds like she is snoring, but I know she is choking. I pass out. Later through the fog I see a nurse, then a flash of a metal hospital syringe, and a minute later the choking is lighter. Mother says something. I know she is not talking to me anymore and I can't make myself wake up.

Somebody shakes me. Let's go, the voice says, and I follow a pair of feet across the cold hospital floor, across the concrete of the park where the lung patients spend their stronger days playing chess or sneaking a cigarette or two. I lie across the backseat until the car stops. I trail behind into my building elevator, then alone into my room, into my bed, and into the darkness under the covers.

. . .

The phone rings twenty times. Everybody knows it is the hospital and nobody wants to answer. I turn over in bed and face the animal carvings in the wall. I dug them out with my finger as a child when I ate plaster every night before I went to sleep. The doctors said I had calcium deficiency and should drink more milk. Aunt Dika made Mother put gloves on my hands at bedtime. Now I scratch the duck shape bigger. The grit scrapes my tooth enamel. The day goes by outside my bedroom.

At dusk Dika comes in and sits next to me.

Hungry?

No.

I roll over and put my head in her lap. She is wearing a dark green dress, and smells like Grandmother, a slower death coming.

What are we going to do? I ask her.

My aunt Dika is a war hero who once destroyed more than a dozen Nazi bunkers, until she was struck with a piece of shrapnel from a German Stuka. Then she was captured, and traded a month later. She has never told anybody what it was like to be a captured pretty girl. I think maybe because no one ever asked. Out of fear, I suppose. Because she always told the truth.

You are going to have to live with your father, she says.

Just like that.

. . .

Mother is buried in a brown, expensive coffin wearing her best silk suit and her snakeskin shoes we bought in Trieste. The graveyard is stark. Muslim graveyards are always stark. No mausoleums for important men. No long lists of devoted wives and children. Nobody from Father's family shows up. He doesn't call. We hate each other, the Aunts explain.

I stand far away while people buzz around me. Do I want anything to eat, to drink? I wish for nothing, except the bottle

I've stashed under my bed, among the old pajamas, out of range of the Aunts' cleaning twisters. I sipped all morning, and smeared my mouth with honey to kill the smell.

The house is menacing in the afternoon. People are going in and out, their bodies covering our furniture, even the corner chairs where no one ever sits. The tables are connected in one long line of food and drinks. The dog sits nervously wagging her tail, hoping to catch some leftovers. The neighborhood women wash the dishes and bring out more food for the new visitors. Everywhere it reeks as if someone were boiling saltwater in a pot and forgot to turn off the stove. The heavy smell of dry tears. I am not staying here. Can't stay here. I will sell my skates, my dolls, my leather jacket. I keep eyeing Mother's diamond pin, wondering how much of the ticket that would pay off.

Two visitors, women who worked with Mother, are leaving the apartment now. They say good-bye and wish me good luck.

Are you taking the bus? the taller one asks her colleague.

No. I think I'll walk. It's a beautiful summer night.

9

The summer heat stirs trouble across the
Balkans. By August there is something
fishy going on in the government. Times
are about to get bad for the Muslims.
Aunts and Uncles meet secretly in the
kitchen. I sneak behind the door and
listen.

There will be bloodshed.

Where?

In Bosnia.

Bosnia?

Where else?

So what? Aunt Dika says. We bled once.

What about Sasha? Malik, the ambassador Uncle, asks.

She failed almost every subject this year. Something has
to be done. Others agree.

I hear the hiss of a match.

We'll send her to her father soon. She can spend the mourning period here, but as soon as it is over we'll send her down to him.

I try to remember how long the mourning period is, and I draw a blank. Then I remember KC and how he said, You are strong. Strong means doing what you have to do.

I use the next-door neighbor's phone to call America. The husband's company pays the bill. I visit when I know he is away. The wife is softhearted and dim. She pities the young girl who has just lost her mother and she rushes into the kitchen for some jam, promises one of her favorite jars. I grab the phone and dial feverishly.

City University, a woman says.

Suddenly I am mild, a sweet girl from a poor country, a sweet girl with a dream. I've just lost my mom, and I would like to come to America, and can you please, please help me?

The lady is quiet. Exhales with compassion.

I am so sorry for your trouble, dear child. I lost my mother too. A wave of panic sloshes through me. I am hungry for more of this nice lady.

Ma'am, my uncles want to put me in the orphanage.

Dear child.

I must get to America.

Goodness. I am not the one who makes those decisions, but I will make sure your application goes out today, I promise. Spell me your last name. I will send it express.

I tell the perfect stranger all the different ways you can spell a strange Eastern European name, many consonants together, and she must hear how scared I am because she tries to comfort me.

Listen, she says. The key is to have funds. You need to have twenty thousand dollars in the bank in order to get the visa. And you need to be eighteen.

Thank you, I say at the end. Thank you for being kind.

I hang up the phone before I hear the kitchen door swing and I am all smiles and thank-yous and hmmms, what a delicious jam this is. You can never buy anything like this in the store. The neighbor's wife smiles. I'm sorry for your loss. She was such a fine woman, a beauty, a lady, your mother.

Too bad I am not like her.

No, no, my child, she says. Don't say such things.

Sorry, I say. I get like that when it's hard.

I understand, she says and turns quiet.

We sit in silence for a while.

How long have you lived here? I ask. I know she is from far away, four hundred miles, which is infinity around here, and was married off after a two-week courtship.

Too long.

Are you happy? I ask.

She looks at me as if she has never seen me before.

Do you want a drink? she asks.

. . .

I open Mother's closets, files, shoe boxes, everything. I have never snooped through anything of Mother's before, but she is gone and they're my closets now. There are drawers filled with school records in different color inks. Mother used different colors to enter her students' first- and second-semester grades. I find a blank high-school diploma. I stop and look at it for a while. I dictated grades to her from the report cards. She wrote them at the bottom of the diplomas. I get an idea. I know how to do this.

Language, A. I was always good at language, even when I was bad at everything else. Math, B; physics, A; chemistry, A. I never had any chemistry. Political science, A. I don't know what political science is. I press Mother's school stamp at the bottom. It's old and dry, but it will have to do. Suddenly I am a very promising high-school graduate.

I find her bankbook inside her favorite purse. It says 350 Swiss francs. Our entire fortune. The zero was entered in black ink with something resembling a stamp. Mother's stamp has no zero. If I could just make two perfect half-circles: press the letter *C* the right way, then turn it around. I spit on the stamp to make the ink darker. It works. I have a zero. I press again. Two zeros. 350 became 35000.

I get my birth certificate. It says that I was born in 1966. Too young to leave the country without my parents' consent. I erase the little curve inside the last number 6. It turns into a letter *C*. Then I spit and turn the *C* on my stamp one more time. And make it a zero. Now I was born in 1960. I am twenty, an excellent student, and an heir to thirty-five thousand Swiss francs, which is more than twenty-five thousand dollars.

The application asks many questions, with many empty lines to fill. Name, date of birth, schools attended. I answer the best that I can, then write a letter of recommendation for myself and pay three kids from the area to sign it. They are my professors. I write a heartbreaking personal essay. At first it's hard to lie, to embellish, but then I pretend I am writing about somebody else. I become Father, and golden words pour out of my pen.

Many generations of Immigrants have tried their luck and dreams as the steaming ships arrived across the Atlantic carrying in very little other then the hopes and dreams of those clutching to the boats edge in anticipation.

It's stupid, but I think they'll like it.

America expanded and become the only nation on the world available to everyone who wanted to do and try his or her best. The only nation where many nations could live united.

Aunt Dika calls America a bunch of racist Protestants exploiting and raping everybody else.

My mother has recently passed away. My father died in a terrible mining accident and left a young widow behind years before. My sister was struck by a scarlet fever.

Since I never had a sister I saw no evil omen in inventing a dead one.

What remains is the memory of her, is the determination she installed in me, the desire to be successful, to be part of the greatest nation in the world. I wish to establish a family of my own, since I have been unfortunately deprived of the biological one.

I show it to my friend who writes a little English.

Damn, she says, this is good. Especially the part about your father and sister dying. I'd believe it if I read it.

. . .

A month later the acceptance letter arrives. I have been officially accepted by the College of Staten Island. It feels strange to go to a college on an island—islands are made for bathing, fishing, and fig eating—but I know everything is different and better in America and I can't wait to see the island school.

The family council won't hear about America. What do you know about the crazy land of exploitation and religious sects? Aunt Dika asks. It's hard there. Try being a Mexican in California. Working endless hours. Aging prematurely.

But I am not going to California, I say. I want to go to New York and I am not Mexican.

She is not listening to me. They'll think you are. She flares her white nostrils. They'll think you are a Mexican from another planet once they see your black eyes and you open your big mouth and they realize you walk on your head with your ass in the clouds and are good for nothing but picking fruit. You better finish some sort of a course, a trade school or something, to put a slice of bread in your pocket one day.

It would crumble, I say, and mess up my clothes.

She grumbles, Ass in the clouds. I throw back, At least mine is small enough to lift in the air, and then Uncle bops me one across the back of my head. Sister, sister, he says to Dika compassionately, she is insolent, stubborn, like that no-good dissident father of hers. There is nothing we can do. Let us make sure she is out of here soon, the bad girl, the rotten apple that bothers and embarrasses us all.

. . .

One must wait in line for a visa. One must come at dawn, or at midnight, and wait. People don't leave the line. We sit on the floor and wait for permission to escape. Some of us are sleeping. Some have been here for two or three days and they smell. They might have traveled from far away with just the clothes they're wearing. They go to the bathroom between the parked cars hoping no one is looking.

A little too old to be going to college, the officer says, reading my birth certificate.

Better late than never, I say politely.

He doesn't look at me, he just leans his narrow head with no hair on the top over my papers and slams approval on my plans.

Multiple entry to the United States of America N380107.

There is no light on in the apartment when I return. I can hear Aunt Dika quietly crying in the bedroom. It's time for Mother's shot. She probably misses being busy, even if it meant digging through Momma's parched veins. Uncle is at the neighbor's, playing cards and not thinking about the dead, and now I too miss her parched veins, and wish she were here, sick and dying, but still here. And I try to coax myself, She is gone, she is gone, turn on the light and look at the old chairs, the familiar shapes, don't be afraid. I lurch into the room, open the closet, and take the suitcase out. What does one pack in secret for forever? Mother's white gloves, the ladylike ones that go all the way up the arm with three pearl buttons, her lovely classy pictures, some of my clothes, and a roll of money, my $2,745 inside a box of "ladies' pads."

. . .

There is always a party when somebody is leaving. The family
and friends gather dutifully. I've just lost my mother, it would
be rude not to. The questions swerve around. Are you going all
alone? Who do you know in America? What do you mean to do
there among the Protestants and the Jews?

Get an education.

Education? You can't get that around here?

Soon everyone is drinking, no longer reluctant to have
a party in a dead woman's house, a dead woman whose wake
they drowned in brandy not two months ago. Our throats are
dry, somebody says. Besides, this is a wake too, the special
kind of wake, a *pečalba* wake, for someone who is leaving for
good. Good riddance, really. The girl is bad and wild, and
maybe there is room for her sort in America, in the crazy
country where women drive and sue their husbands for
divorce. Maybe in the crazy America there will be room for
this crazy girl.

Živeli, Uncle cheers at me for the first time in his life.

I am encouraged. I want him to like me. I want him to
think me one of them, even if only once, even if this is the
last time. I take his revolver and empty the charger out the
window.

Let's dance, I scream.

Dance, the drunken room replies, and the music blasts.

My family and friends grab one another's hands, form a
circle, and start following the music filled with sadness and
anger. The thump of the bass warns of the coming of the
enemy. It makes the brave warriors thirsty for the enemies'
blood, and they drink more to kill the thirst, but the thirst

resists. The brandy never kills it. It grows stronger and stronger in their bellies until they all get a chance to kill for real.

The neighbors are piled against their windowpanes crossing themselves and disapproving. The neighbor's wife is crying. She's been avoiding me in the stairwell, perhaps embarrassed about the drinks we had, the secrets we shared about the unhappiness of her life.

I spit at them. What the fuck are you staring at, I scream in English, and wave the gun.

Stop it, Aunt Dika scorns. We have to live with them.

I don't.

Father shows up almost at the end of the evening, uninvited. I didn't even know he was back. Immediately, he offers to carve the pig, as if he were the head of this house he wasn't allowed inside of until today. I let him. He prances around the table, offering beer and brandy to everybody, making sure everybody's plate is full of everything we have to offer. After dinner he is dancing with one of my friends' girlfriends. His hand is too low on her back. She is beaming like the Glyfada girls do when a newly arrived GI picks them first. It is a look of promise, of hope. I am happy for Father. I am happy for Secca, who is about to learn many things about the magnificent past of his beloved Greece. Soon her frenzied boyfriend is looking for her everywhere.

I scream *Yihhaa* out the window into a quiet Socialist night. The police car is downstairs, but it would be a few years before Uncle would be stripped of his rank. For now they are only observing, making sure we, the dirty Muslims, don't get completely out of hand.

The Serbs at the party huddle closer. The patriotic songs

are about to start. Brandy pours down. Tears of pride follow. The Serbian men are pledging to freedom. It's on its way. Sweet Freedom. Sweet Victory. Long live Serbia. More tears of pride stream down their faces, and they hug one another— Brother, for you I would kill anybody; for you and for our beloved Serbia—and they hug one another some more and sing and cry. Uncle whispers, Animals. In my sister's house. Disgrace. We'll see about their Serbia. We'll just have to see.

In the morning, the television and a piece of the wall are missing; somebody has taken a hammer and knocked out part of it. Had to have been Marko, the one boasting of nationalism the most, and of the soon-to-be-rightfully-restored Christian right to pillage Muslim women. He is in love with Leila, who is Muslim and I think a piece of shit. There is always something of a snake in her air. Or some other reptile. As I grab Mother's fancy white Samsonite suitcase and leave forever, a nasty thought of Leila doing a number on him flashes through my head. She will. Three years later, when the last of the Muslims leave Belgrade, she will be holding on to the hand of a son Marko will never know. A steep payment for some torn off cement, a black-and-white TV set, and a lot of bragging? Maybe. But by then Marko will have long volunteered to serve in the Serbian special units called the Red Berets, responsible for a lot more than my wall.

. . .

I stop at the Mental Building to say good-bye to Juma. The family's kept the news about Mother's death away from her. She hasn't been sleeping. She stopped sleeping and reading the *Britannica* after she returned from Cuba. She just sits by the window. Aunt Ludmila says the orderlies don't even lock her door anymore.

Take me with you, she says with her back turned to me.

How did you know it was me? I ask.

Who else could it be?

I can't take you, I say.

I know, America is for the strong.

I am sorry, I say.

Don't be. You don't have to live here.

Part

THREE

10

The storm comes. It assails. Envelops. It
screeches underneath and above howls,
drums. It blows in colors, scents, shapes,
shrieks, sirens, and sounds, sounds
everywhere. Millions of faces scurry by,
frantic for refuge.

New York City.

My future landlord, Dragutin, waits for me at the airport.
A friend gave me the name of somewhere I could stay for
cheap if I don't mind sharing a bed. With a girl, of course. He
even picks you up, the friend said. For three dollars, which is
nothing. The car is bigger than a sheep corral and I wish I
could lie across the backseat.

On Victory Street in Ridgewood, Queens, we enter a
square, gray, and ugly three-story building shoved tightly
between similar gray and ugly buildings. Garbage escapes
the black bags in front of the building. The air smells of

stale animal cages. The steps are uneven and aslant, creaky. I love it all, even the garbage.

Dragutin is Romanian. To escape Communism, he swam across the Danube gripping a tractor wheel he stole from his neighbors. He walked two hundred miles to the American Embassy and asked for asylum. Later he sent money for a new wheel via some returning Romanians. It was a sign for his village that he'd made it to the other side.

I wake the next morning to him screaming at the homeless Spanish for pissing and worse outside the building. Disgusting, he grunts. Back in the old country even the poorest were honorable enough not to disrespect the hardworking good folks' property.

Dragutin has strong forearms and does push-ups every morning in front of an open window. His girlfriend is a licensed facialist in Manhattan. She makes a bundle, he says. American ladies insist on Eastern European facials. They sleep in the first room of a railroad apartment he purchased for cash after only nine years in America. I share the next room with the girl, who is from my country. The charge is fifty dollars a week. For this we get to shower once, well, he grumbles, twice a week, if we absolutely need to. He disapproves of the length of my hair and the amount of hot water needed to rinse it. I always take cold showers, he challenges. Good for the blood. We get scrambled pale-yolked, tasteless eggs Saturday and Sunday mornings, and we have to do the dishes and wash the bathroom on Saturday afternoons.

My roommate, Irene, is resolute and rigid. The bed we share has a big brown stain. She heaps her hair on top of her head, pinned like an old woman's, and never laughs. She wraps her clothes inside plastic bags. Green bags for sweaters and shirts, white for pants, socks, and underwear. There are pretty boxes on top of her counter. I peek in when she isn't around. They are empty.

We keep things clean around here. She eyes my jumbled suitcase carefully.

I'll try.

Irene has a plan with a firm destination. She will stay in the United States, carve out a better life for herself and possibly someday for her brother. He too does push-ups in front of an open window, she tells us at dinner.

Smart boy, Dragutin approves. Sure would like to meet him.

God willing, Irene says.

They both frown when I drink Guinness with breakfast. It displeases Jesus.

I'll tell him I'm sorry when I see him, I say.

The nights drag. Irene sleeps with the same determination with which she folds her clothes, never turning, never tossing. Her legs conquer the sheets. Her arms secure the cover. Her breath is always even. Some nights she rustles her money before she turns the light off. Then she hides it inside the belt she never takes off. She never says good night.

Sometimes there is a small rumble in the front room. Always short, always the same. Dragutin shrieks a little, the girlfriend is quiet. The bedsprings screech. Across the hall, I see Dragutin's dark shadow open the bathroom door and turn on the light. I hear the water in the sink. The toilet flushes. The girlfriend stays in bed until the morning.

11

I walk around the city, alone. I walk up
and down the straight, sterile midtown
streets, across one way, back the other.
Always alone. I am worn out from being
alone, worn out by the stain on my
mattress, my roommate's even-paced
breath, her folded sweaters, perfectly
ironed underwear. At night I chomp
through packs and packs of gum and let
saliva roll out the side of my mouth and
onto the pillow, trying to hoax myself into
believing I'm asleep.

In the morning, Dragutin punishes me with his mantra—
Get a job, you must have a job—as his powerful, provider's
forearms carry his confident hands through the air. Work is
what makes us human.

The whole house seems to agree, a job is a good thing. I

try to understand the point. I sit on the stairs of a humongous downtown building and drink beer with bourbon. Silver wheels hit the puddles in front of me, children hold their parents' hands while crossing the street, the responsible gentlemen adjust their ties before speaking.

Help Wanted, the paper promises as it marks my fingers with lead. Make hundreds of dollars working at the Pink Pussy Cat. The innuendo misses me, and I dial the number. A woman with a voice box burned from years of shouting shouts, Are you twenty-one and do you have anything against working with sexual paraphernalia?

No, I lie, and Yes, I say, wondering what *paraphernalia* means. Do I have to touch anybody? I ask.

No.

Do they get to touch me?

No.

Fine, then.

The job pays eight dollars an hour plus commission. The shop is narrow and deep and stacked with rows of sex toys. I've never seen any of them before, and they are mostly funny-looking.

A short girl with a face round like a birthday cake is stuffing an executioner's mask with pink wrapping paper in order to make it look fuller. Or scarier, I guess, on display. She looks uninterested in me, and curses when a small piece of paper gets caught in the zipper that runs across the mouth slit. A videotape with a picture on the box of a blond woman with hardened breasts bending over sells for fifty dollars. She has smeared red makeup across her ass and it looks like a pair of baboon cheeks.

After he finds out where I am from, the owner, Eddie, introduces himself as a Communist who believes that power to the people comes through sexual liberation. I make no comment. I have no social security number and I don't want to cause any trouble.

Eddie asks me to rub some K-Y on the dildos, says he needs to know if I have what it takes to make the dough for him. I am afraid to touch them at first. They look pale and unhealthy, lined up like sick children at the doctor's office.

The only thing that bothers me is the smell, so I rub them up and down and wait for more instructions. He tells me, Don't forget the balls.

I obey and get a job.

*   *   *

KC's friend Spivey is suspicious. I try reassuring him with memories. How KC fell over the fence at P.S. 104 and landed on Spivey's head. How Spivey later claimed KC gave him a brain concussion and used it as an excuse for not taking the math test. He is still nervous.

How long did you know him? he asks.

A year. I was his girlfriend when things turned sour with Lisa.

You're not a cop, are you?

No. I'm the one who found him at the table.

The silence is long.

What's your name? he says gently.

Sasha.

I'll meet you at Schulman's on 125th tonight at nine P.M.

.   .   .

The bar is long and narrow, with neatly spread-out ashtrays and red leather bar stools. I am the only white person. The bartender, a tall man with a long blue apron, sizes me up without offering a drink. An old shipwreck of a man leans into the table underneath the stage, his hat resting next to his mug. His hands shake; his nails have surrendered and they grow turned in to his fingers. A woman sits a few tables down with her back to him. She has enormous breasts, the kind you would step out of the way to avoid running into. She's wearing a red hat with a feather and netting. There are pictures of black blues and jazz stars on the walls. I recognize some that KC taught me. The cool cats, he said. Cool as shit, like my baby.

Then another man enters. Almost as old as Father. He looks at me, his eyes narrow.

It is me, I say.

You're a child.

You're ancient.

After we get over our surprise, he offers me a drink. The bartender makes his first trip over to this side of the bar.

What do you want? Spivey asks.

What'll you have?

Hennessy.

KC liked Hennessy too.

I taught him that, he says, and looks at the empty ashtray.

I miss him too, I say.

Let's have some Hennessy, then.

We toast to KC and Spivey turns around and faces the bar.

This place and I go back.

I know about places like that, I say.

How old are you? He smiles.

Old enough.

The lady with a hat gives us an angry look.

She's KC's friend from Greece, Spivey tells her. Not that it's any of your business.

What? She jumps up and rushes toward us, almost losing her hat. Why didn't you tell me right away? she scorns Spivey.

Still angry? Spivey asks her.

That fool, she says, dead and buried for the benefit of one white girl. And here sits another one.

Oh, shut up, Ethel, Spivey says. She was his girl. Ethel turns quiet and Spivey whispers, Sorry for her crap. She loved KC.

We all did, she says, and want to know all the details.

I tell them everything. How I found him, and how there was vomit on baby K's diapers. They learn about Cole from Paducah, western Kentucky, and his crossing the Mississippi and winning the lawn-mower race. Good for my brother, Spivey says. I tell them about Father and his rich girlfriend who lived on the top floor and had neatly stacked kindling next to her fireplace, and how Mother was in a coma when I last saw her, and how she was so worried about me, and how she doesn't have to worry anymore.

Ethel cries and kicks the chair. Fucking life, she says. What the fuck for?

Spivey tells me, She was real close to KC when they was kids, and she never forgave him for Lisa, and don't be mad at her.

I'm not mad, I say.

Is there something we can do for you? Ethel asks. James

over there—she points at the old man—will sing you any song. Is there a song you'd like to hear?

"Strange Fruit," I say.

You are a strange girl, she tells me.

And the old man wails Billie's song for me, song of the sad Billie whose name KC said never to use for my daughter, and my head hangs with tears and Hennessy, and Ethel's colossal brown cleavage moves toward me, and I am held. Don't cry baby, this too shall pass, that is just how things are, life is hard that way.

Fucking life, I say to the empty ashtray.

12

The girl with the birthday-cake face is
Sheila. She came to the Pink Pussy Cat
when she was nineteen, and stayed. Now
she is the manager. She knows where
everything is, and works the register
faster than anyone else. She was engaged
once, she tells me, to an Irish guy, but his
family objected to her parents' divorce,
her brother in jail, and her disreputable
job. After they lived together for a year the
boyfriend finally gave in to his parents
and the whole thing fell apart. Now she
wears black nail polish and her eyes are
sad. During her break she sits in the back
and adds more coats of polish. It's too
thick inside the bottle, that's why it chips,
I want to tell her, but I don't know how to
start.

The next day, I bring the polish remover, and show her how to thin it.

Thank you, she says. If you want to take your break early, you can.

Let me do your nails, I say. I used to do it with my mom and my aunts all the time.

We sit in the back under the shelf stacked with dildos and strawberry-flavored edible underwear. Those are our best-selling items. Sheila is minuscule and almost disappears in the chair. She bites the skin around her nails. I show her how to push the cuticles back, and tell her to make sure she gives the first coat a few minutes.

Does this hurt? I point at the raw skin.

I don't know why he left me, she says, looking at her skin. I'm not my mother. I've had the same job for years. I don't owe any money, I'm a manager. I don't even smoke.

Must be hard, I say.

You're a nice girl.

As her nails dry she asks if I want to eat dinner together, but the new videos arrive and since she's the only one with the key for the video closet, we have to eat in shifts while they are being delivered.

. . .

Eddie never sticks around the shop. I trust my Sheila, he says. Since she's been a manager things are pretty tight around here. He goes into the back office for a moment, makes a phone call, snorts some coke, and leaves.

Before he steps out he orders us to leave the radio on a

soft-rock station. Shitty music makes it easier for people to relax, he says. We don't want the customers thinking. We want them to have fun.

Eddie is right. The music seems to do the trick. The happy couples smile ooh and ahh in front of the dildo-filled cases, especially the couples who are here only to gawk. Down here from their nice houses tucked away somewhere called Darien or Rye. Is this underwear really edible? a man asks. What kind of people buy this kind of stuff? A girlfriend pretends to be bashful. If the couple is really preppy and the girl is blond, Sheila will jangle her many store keys on her chain, roll her eye-linered eyes, and stab them with a look: Are you fucking buying or are you wasting my time here jerking me off?

Then there are the boys from Jersey. Too young to go to bars and drown their fears. Their blank faces are covered with thin hair and bad-diet pimples, their inexperienced cheeks crimson. I'm the only one who doesn't mind their silly teased hair. Everybody else hates Jersey. It's the pits, Sheila says. If the boys get rowdy, she stomps over to the S&M section and pulls on one of the nipple-clamp chains. This is what you need for your dick, she says, except I may have to look for it with a magnifying glass. Get out of here before I call security.

Security is a drag queen from New Orleans named Sally. We are friends from the first moment we meet and in less than a week we have a routine. During our break we sip scotch from paper cups and puff on a tightly rolled joint. I tell her about KC, Mother, Uncle, even Cousin. Her eyes get teary.

Fuck! she says. I am glad I don't have to be a man anymore. The whole world's gone to hell.

We drink more and play my first Maceo Parker CD, which

she gave me for my birthday. It is my only birthday present. Sometimes she tells me stories of the aging Big Easy drags, who've lost their shine just like Bourbon Street and are rotting slowly in the thick air of Louisiana marshes. She tells me to stay away from white-boy music and to never wear blue. It clashes with your skin. Red. Red is your hot color.

Sally steals from the store every day. I think Eddie knows. How many extra-extra-large teddies can go missing in one week without anyone noticing? It seems the two have some sort of a deal between them. Sally goes out with a plastic surgeon who gave Eddie a great deal on his last girlfriend's breast enlargement. Thank God, Eddie says, a man can finally look forward to seeing them in the light.

I steal too. It's easy. I don't ring up an item, I just put it in the bag for the customer and the money goes in the register. I keep a tally in my head and after every hour or two I take the extra cash from the register. It's easy. The actual buying customers want to get away as quickly as possible. Especially the couples in nice clothes. They never use a charge card, although the imprint says only LPPD Ltd.

. . .

Our house in Queens is soaked, soaped, and scrubbed before the holidays while the suckling pig waits to be roasted in the oven. Its dead gaping mouth, the stench of bleach burning the tiles, and the sweat on Dragutin's broad forehead as he lugs in his freshly purchased kill, all of it, makes me ill.

The Pussy Cat is closed but Sally invited me to a party at her friend Armando's and promised a straight crowd so that at least I will have fun.

The empty subway car rushes over elevated tracks. A dozing man's head is haloed first by a fluorescent rum billboard with an inviting woman, then by the shiny decorated trees, then by the houses with families congregating behind opened curtains. He has a hunter's hat on, with flaps that droop over his ears, and a tear in his right shoe.

Merry Christmas, I tell him.

Christmas, he says back.

Armando's apartment is on the first floor inside the Avenue D projects. The music is Spanish and the house is crammed. There are brothers, cousins, aunts, uncles, second cousins, friends, neighbors. Two fat ladies occupy the entire couch, with a small man winking constantly perched in between them like a lapdog.

I am not sure whose boyfriend the guy is, Sally says. The fat lady on the left murmurs something about the right way of celebrating the first day sweet baby Jesus graced the world with his presence, and not with all this commotion. The man winks in approval. Nobody speaks to me, so I sit on the floor and lean my murky head against the cold wall and wait. I remember Mother for a second, whimper, and hit my head against the wall. I miss her, miss her, and the pounding does nothing to quiet the craving. Where are you? I ask the carpet, the chairs, the feet and shoes passing. Nobody answers.

The party racket is mounting. More people come in. The two fat women rise to leave, almost carrying their little boyfriend afloat between them. I go to the kitchen seeking alcohol. There are pictures on the refrigerator. Boys in red life vests and a girl, looking terrified, holding the hand of a giant mouse. I take two beers and return to the people dancing in the middle of the living room. The flickering lights draw figures on their faces. I find the bathroom. A pencil-thick light ray shines under the door. Somebody is inside.

I walk downstairs and outside the building. It's late, but it's a warm, dry Christmas night. The playground next to the project is childless and dark. The abandoned seesaw lurks over the sandbox. A security car parked next to the entrance seems empty. The gate screeches as I open it. I sit on a swing and sip my beer.

The gate screeches again. A blond-haired guy with an oval face sits on the swing next to me.

Merry Christmas, he says.

Yeah, I say.

Too many people in there? he asks.

But the beer is good.

Are you Armando's friend?

Was supposed to meet him, but the crowd's too much. Here. I offer him my spare bottle.

He smiles, and the small creases next to his blue eyes remind me of Mother and the good things in life.

You're beautiful, I say. What's your name?

Scott, he says. Come, I'll buy you a drink somewhere else.

Where?

There's a great bar close by.

Which bar? I know all the bars, I say.

King Tut's Wa Wa Hut.

I've never been inside the Hut. Nobody but white junkies go there. We walk by the bouncer, who is sitting on a chair nodding. Scott goes straight for the jukebox. It makes me nervous. I want him close, so I pin my eyes to his back until he is lost in the crowd. A shimmering picture of Jesus' head, crowned with thorns, hangs over the bar. I take a step. Jesus winks at me. Now he has a beard, a golden tooth, and a grin.

Can I help you? the bartender, a tall and slender girl, asks me.

What do you call that? I point behind her.

Booze, she says.

I mean the one above, winking?

Jesus.

Scott comes back and I realize he's not much taller than me, and I wonder if he'd let me wear his black silver-tipped cowboy boots.

Your hair looks like chocolate in this light, he says.

Thanks, I say.

How about some pool? he asks.

How about some drugs?

He pulls a large pill from his pocket.

What's this? I ask.

Good stuff.

Where did you get those boots? I ask.

South America.

Which one?

He studies my face for a while.

Where did you come from? he asks.

The same place as the pill.

It takes weeks before we kiss. He says he wants to know me, says he is afraid of things moving too fast. I don't understand, but I love being around him, listening to the sound of his words, so I wait. He does dope only a few times a week, keeps it under control that way, he says, and his apartment is teeny. Only one room, with a refrigerator and a dirty stove with a TV set on top of it. I eat out, he says, which means at restaurants. His mattress is clean but caved. He inherited it from a roommate who checked into rehab after they lost their old apartment. Their rent was five months overdue, and the landlord was trying to get rid of everybody, so Scott packed his clothes in a plastic bag and split. The next day, he snuck back in, looking for forgotten CDs. The place was ransacked already. Except the mattress. It sat by itself in the middle of the apartment. He thought it was a sign so he dragged it over from Orchard Street.

I love it, I say, and run my hand over the sheetless surface. It's narrow and we sleep diagonally, in each other's laps, on the first night he lets me stay over.

I love your skin and all your moles, he says.

They are blemishes, I say.

They're perfect blemishes.

His body is frail, almost like a girl's. His chest is pale, hairless, and flat, not muscular, as if bound by a long childhood disease. His stomach line is slightly wider than his hips. He wants to look in my eyes when we finally make love. I can't do it, and it clouds his face. His sex is gentle, slow, and soft, looking for direction. When he is finished he falls asleep, curled up and sad. I caress his cheeks, like Mother did mine when I was good, except my hands smell like K-Y jelly, and I tell him, Don't worry, I am here now.

. . .

Scott kisses me in public. He calls me lovely and introduces me as his girlfriend. It feels unusual not to have to hide.

Sometimes I am proud of it, sometimes I hate it. Sometimes both. People smile at us. Nice couple, they say. Even if we are strung out.

On his paydays he takes me to restaurants with his friends. I sit next to nice people who want to know about me. What was it like growing up with Communism? We did the best that we could, I say. They believe everything, and focus their gullible faces that know no hardship. They talk about their parents. How they try to stop them from expressing their real inner selves. I don't understand a word, but I think they are wonderful.

They ask if I have left anyone behind. I think of Father and tell a story. I was little, I say, when my father, a famous professor, first told me about how Helios's horses carry the sun in the back of his carriage, which is why he shines so bright. At the end of the day, they slow down, tired, and bow their heads. And how Apollo is the god of gods who makes brave men confront their guilt. The god of gods, they repeat. Everybody thinks I am smart. Scott is proud of his girlfriend. They ask if I have ever had sushi. Yes, I lie. The food comes and I'm upset. Not because it's raw fish, but because I lied. I always lie now. And it's easy.

At night if I am not stoned, I panic. A weight presses against my chest and I want to wake Scott and whisper into his sleeping face that I am horrible. Instead I stumble to the kitchen and have a drink and wait for the alcohol to drive the tears out. They drop in the glass. Some nights solace is slow in coming. I reach for the hand mirror we use for lines. After I lick it clean I check Scott's breathing and I cry again with

relief as he fogs the surface. I don't want anything to happen
to him. I don't want him to be hurt or cold or scared. I tuck
him in, and if his toes are cold I blow on them until they are
warmer. I don't even think I love him, and still I'm afraid I'll
bring him the bad luck I carry around. Sometimes he wakes
up and wipes what he calls the nose tears, and hugs me and
rocks me and whispers, I love you, lovely, until the stupor
takes over and I pass out.

Everything is easier in the morning. He never asks about,
never mentions, the night before. We pretend it didn't
happen and we go back to being a girlfriend and a boyfriend.
He is never angry. I tell him nothing about myself, just jokes
from the store. I think I hurt him with my silence and he
turns his long, frail back to me while he's sleeping. The
narrow vertebrae protrude through his white skin like
Mother's. Then I hug him, tell him, *Te amo*, don't be angry.
Even when he says he's not angry, he turns his back to me
again. I hold him from behind and breathe into the hair at the
back of his neck. I know he is sad about us. He says, I know
you won't stay. He doesn't say it's because I can't be with only
one man, like KC did, but he is younger than KC and not as
smart. He just kisses the inside of my elbow and whispers,
You can't, there is so much of you. Who could ever keep up? I
don't understand, but I know he means what he's saying. I'll
stay, I whisper, I promise. He smiles. I'll try, I say. Then, if we
don't have money for dope, we drink Jägermeister, huddle,
and try to feel warm.

I never officially moved in with Scott, or left Queens. One
night, totally stoned, I snuck out with Mother's suitcase in my

hands. Irene jumped up and grabbed her money belt, assessed my suitcase, and told me I'd be damned. I shrugged my shoulders and closed the door.

At Scott's, I don't unpack the ladylike white Samsonite, I just shove it behind the door. Scott seems happy with me there. Tells me things are as they should be. For a while I pretend he is right. He goes to work every other morning. When he comes back, I am either still in front of the TV or I am getting ready to go to the Pink Pussy Cat for my shift, and I always forget to ask him how his day has been. I promise I will next time, I will be a good girlfriend to my sweet Scott. But when he comes home and smiles at me, and always brings me something, I am so happy to see him, I forget my promise.

. . .

There is another apartment across the hall. Ace and his mess, Scott says. We can hear them fighting when we come home and stop to unlock the door. The girl is Dominican, Scott says, from another one of the island countries between the two Americas. She is pretty and short. One night I run into her walking alone down the stairs, wearing a gold lamé dress, and I say, *Hola*. She looks away. I figure she's embarrassed and doesn't know I'm just off the boat and poor, despite my *gringo* boyfriend. A boy lives with them, looks like he could be her son, but I can't tell if Ace is the father. They also have a little dog that they never let out.

Ace is friendly with Scott. I hate him the moment I see him. He reminds me of Monica's Larry and I ask him if he's from north Florida when I meet him. He is indignant: north

Florida? Gee, nothing but niggers and rednecks in north Florida. No, baby, I am a cultured gentleman from Georgia.

Ace is a pimp. The boy's mother works for him. He has two more girls in Queens, but they are strung out on crack and no longer profitable in Manhattan, he complains. He used to be able to take all three shopping every day. No other pimp in this neighborhood does that much for his girls. Fuck, what a kind heart he has, he even bought them fake birth certificates down South, and is working on their green cards. The girl is illegal and doesn't speak English. I don't believe a word he's saying, but have no way of explaining it to her.

Their working routine is simple. They leave around ten. Ace pays the superintendent's wife to take care of the boy. He doesn't fall asleep easily and she stays with him until he does. Then she carries him downstairs and keeps him there. The nights I can't sleep, I hear Ace and the girl returning around four. The front door opens. They knock on the super's door and wait for a while. Then Ace hops up the rest of the stairs and the girl comes up slowly on her stilettos, balancing the little sleeping body. Ace never helps.

If the girl has a visit from a regular john, Ace comes over and gets high with us. The boy goes out to play in the school yard. Ace complains how all three girls have not been working steadily lately and he is practically broke, taking care of everybody's hospital bills.

Fucking crack is destroying me, man. They like it more than anything. Even more than the dick in the ass. This country is going down the drain with it, I'm telling you, and there's not enough money in the government to fight it.

You're right, Scott agrees.

I tell you, I can't remember the last time all three of them went to work together. Fucking pain, feeding them for nothing.

When we run out of beer he gives Scott a twenty to buy more. As soon as Scott's feet hit the concrete outside the apartment Ace starts in on me. You, he grins and sizes me up and down, with your straight back and your proud eyes, you're a whole other ball game altogether. Raised to be a lady. I can tell. I'd get some classy Madison Avenue clothes for you and send you off to an expensive hotel. You'd make thousands.

How much would I get to keep? I ask.

Come on, you know the drill. I keep the money and we go shopping every day.

You're a motherfucker, I say.

I'm just a businessman. I'd buy you T-bills every month or two, like I did for my girls before they fucked up. Then you can retire someday. You can't be on the street for the rest of your life.

13

The only tree on our street blossomed too
early, duped by the week of good weather
that followed the New Year, and now, in
April, it's bald without any buds. I pour
some warm beer into the little square of
soil apportioned to the tree and hope it
doesn't die.

I am sitting on the stoop drinking and watching the
people whiz by. Music plays from several parked cars. It
clashes but it keeps my mind busy. The homeless are pro-
testing some homeless business, surrounded by their rich
would-be saviors who come down from their uptown homes.
None of them is here at night.

A girl sits next to me, a beautiful, mysterious girl I
instantly want to know. Round and perfect. Tender white skin
rolls up and down her arms. Even on young people you can
see in which direction the skin will stretch. How it will lose its

youth. Heather's is directionless. Just sprawling softness, inviting touches, kisses. The day we met was the best I ever remembered her looking. She peaked that afternoon. Men passing on the street sense it too: They change. Their backs tighten, their chests lift. She laughs at them and talks about something but I am not listening. Her red curls falling all over her smoothness are making me woozy. I want her. I want her to want me. I want Scott to have her. I want KC to be here and pontificate in front of this miracle of nature until she wants him like I did. I must have her. Every fiber of my being organizes itself toward her. I too sit up.

What is your name? I ask.

Heather is a southerner and a stripper. Calls it a belle-tease. I laugh. There is no touching or any other gross stuff, and the money is good. I share Despina's full-release story. Yikes, she shudders, heavy. Having kids is hard. Makes you do shit. My stage name is Jessica Rabbit, you know, the red hair. You should try it, she tells me. You could make a fortune with those boobs and curves.

. . .

Later that night, our first night, at someone's birthday party at Alcatraz, she sings "Happy Birthday, Mr. President" and takes her top off to show me how easy it is. I knew her nipples would be small and pink. The flashing yellow Corona sign shining from the cracked front window turns them orange. Then pink again. Then orange. I put my fingers close to them and make a shadow of a duck. Then a rabbit.

Alcatraz was broken into last night and only cheap bottles

were left. A pro hit, the bouncer tells us. Russians: they were looking for the expensive shit, so we have to drink the cheap scotch.

While the crowd gets lost in Heather's body, I filch a bottle of 100 Pipers and we go to her apartment. She lives with her boyfriend, Howie. The three of us split the two bags of heroin I have, and she wants to show me how she dances onstage. Just like you're fucking somebody, she says. It's really easy and the perverts love it. They throw money at you like crazy. Howie doesn't mind, she says, and pulls his pants down. Don't be shy, she tells me, he's limp from the dope, he can't do anything.

Howie is in a band called Blitzpear, which is something in German, although he is from Jersey. He smokes Gitanes and when I tell him I am part Gypsy he says I am full of shit, with no accent, for all he knows I am probably from Nebraska and my name is Jane.

Jane, Jane, that should be your stage name, Heather laughs, and she pulls me over between her legs. It's strange to feel a woman like that with my fingers, although I have felt myself many times. She is warm and tastes like soap and I understand why men long to be inside of her.

We have eggs in the morning. Scrambled for me, omelet for Heather. Call me Jessica when there's nobody around, she says. It turns me on. I say, Jessica, and we kiss. Howie sleeps through breakfast. He can't handle scotch, she says. Plus he sleeps a lot. Otherwise he'd be too boring.

Howie, Scott, Heather, and I spend our mornings, after-noons, and evenings, sometimes two days, at our place or their place. The windows on the building outside reflect the light from the day passing. We snort and drink, and sometimes watch Heather and Howie go at it. If we want to. If we are tired of them, we gossip about his flabby belly and her skin reddened by the rug rashes and how watching people have sex is exciting only the first time, like a brand-new porno. After a while it's dreary and you know exactly when he or she is going to come. Then we know it's time to watch TV and we ask them to keep it quiet. Some days Heather brings Kevin, this gorgeous San Francisco former junkie who is after her, and Howie doesn't seem to mind. Heather's dancing pays for everything and Howie lets him stick around as long as he keeps his hands off. I am jealous of Kevin. If he's persistent he'll steal her. His stories are supercool. He was adopted from Venezuela or Costa Rica or he is part one thing or the other, the details always change. His real mother was a beautiful prostitute. His dad was a Dutch pirate. He sits with us as we do dope and tells us about his father and his infamous schooner that terrorized the coast near Caracas. We all know it's a bunch of bull, except, maybe, that his mother was hot, but the dope is good, and so is his story.

. . .

For a few months that summer we were inseparable. Friends and lovers. Our summer. Heather was the first girl I kissed. Her hairless mouth was maddening. When I traced it with my lips the first time, I thought of Mother and Len and wondered if Len had managed to keep herself out of jail. A cold hunch sliced through my gut and the answer was—no.

. . .

Years later, while I was trying to be a wife, I walked by a sex shop, which I had by then learned to be shocked by. I saw Heather on the cover of a gang-bang video. She was strung out and broken-looking, but still dazzling to me. I waited for my husband to walk on a bit and give us some privacy, leaned in, and kissed the dirty glass.

. . .

At work I sneak into the bathroom and snort a little every half hour. When I am finished I look in the mirror at my eyes, the color of drying mud. I can no longer steal cash. Can't keep the tally in my head. I steal stock instead and give all the spoils to Heather. She sells most of it to girls at the clubs where she dances. She sells it half price and they send their thanks via Jessica Rabbit: Tell that nice friend of yours she's cool.

Sheila figures everything out. She stops talking to me, stops eating with me. I know the job won't last, so I grab as many teddies as I can, the glue-on nipple stars, the furry handcuffs, and I don't even bother to close my bag anymore. Sally turns away when I leave with my backpack stuffed, but I can see she worries about me.

It takes Eddie another month to catch on. You little cunt, he seethes. I think he even wants to hit me, but he is too much of a pussy. Not only because I'm stronger. If I fought back, he knows Sally wouldn't do a thing to help him. Eddie tells me, Bitch, you're fired, give me the keys. Keep the keys, I throw back, everybody I know has a set. The locks are expensive and he almost really takes a swing. I don't flinch, though, and he backs off.

Now cash my check, I say.

And to my surprise he does.

Sally is standing at the door, pissed. Some Puerto Rican boys just passed by and harassed her. She had to get really rough with one of them and show the little punk you can't fuck around with a southern brother even if he's got nice tits. He says, Now, this business with your leaving, and fucking Eddie being a dickhead like he always is. We go into the backyard behind the Slaughtered Lamb, smoke a joint, and wait for her to calm down.

What are you going to do now? she asks.

I'll be all right.

Where are you going to live?

With that boy I hang out with.

Which boy?

This white boy I know.

So that's why you're so fucked up. You with a white boy? It would never work.

No, I think this one's cool.

Another one bites the dust, she says.

What's that supposed to mean?

I never thought you'd disappear into the white world.

Jesus, Sally, he's cool. I'll keep in touch.

No, you won't. Shit, baby, I'm getting a bad feeling about you doing too much dope hanging out with some white guy.

The pot's making you paranoid.

I don't think so.

Whatever.

There you go, already talking like a white girl.

When I am ready to go she gets all teary-eyed and pulls me into her arms. Listen, she says, don't forget three things—

wear red at Mardi Gras, pray for me, and listen to James
Brown.

That man's just too noisy. I wink and leave her life.

. . .

Heather is disappointed that the goods are cut off, and tells
me that if I stripped I could make five times what I made at
the Pink Pussy Cat. What difference does it make, she says
and laughs. You walk around dressed like a hooker anyway.
Stripping means taking your dress and your bra off while on
the stage, or while standing on the bar where guys are having
drinks. In New Jersey you are allowed to stand on the bar with
both legs, but the top has to stay on and the money sucks.
Guys give you dollar bills as tips. They slip them in your
underwear. Sometimes they ask to see more, guys are shit like
that, Heather warns, but for that they have to give you bigger
bills. Don't do it for a five, either. For a ten, show them a little
hair.

I get an audition at the booking agency. Heather and I walk
over to the Flat Iron Building on Twenty-third Street. We
never go this far uptown. Nosebleed, she says. The elevator is
small and smelly and soft inside. The hallway seems narrower
on the top, but I know I am imagining it. The office has piles
of folders dumped everywhere and pictures of famous
baseball players on the walls. Jimmy, the head of the agency,
is on the phone. He waves me in, and Heather waits outside.

Who are you? he asks.

I called.

Name?

Sasha.

Stage or real?

I forgot Heather told me I have to have a stage name.

Stage, I improvise.

A good one. Sexy. Sounds Russian. Where are you from?

Nebraska. My name is Jane.

I don't care what your real name is, let's see what you look like.

I take my sweater off slowly and wish I had a shirt or something else with buttons or a zipper. Dope helps with not being nervous, but it's a normal day outside the window and this is a respectable building.

Jimmy looks away from my nipples. Brown is not his favorite color.

Turn around, he orders.

He studies the curve in my back and grins as if he had some sort of a revelation he was particularly proud of and says, Gordon's.

I've heard of Gordon's. It's a strip joint, far out in Jamaica, Queens. The owner is Greek. Peter, I never caught his last name, has lived in Queens for thirty-five years and has kept himself away from Manhattan for thirty-two. As a young immigrant from Greece he worked as a garbageman in Manhattan, and once got into a bar brawl with some Italians who wouldn't make good on a bet. They beat him senseless and left him inside a garbage can all smeared with shit. Peter swore never to cross the bridge into the city, unless one of his children, and only one of the male ones, was caught in a fire in one of those awful buildings.

He marvels at how fluent my Greek is, *Den pistevo*, can't believe it, are you sure you're not Greek? You lived in Glyfada? No! What a pretty accent you have. What does your father do? Jesus, he is concerned, why is a good, pretty girl like that, *omorfoula*, with a professor father, going down in this way? What he says hurts, but I don't let him know it. Down in which way, I laugh. You mean having more fun than your daughters? His enjoyment abruptly ends. I have just broken the ancient rule—no mention of respectable women in public, and especially not by the unrespectable ones. Even if Pericles, the best of all Greeks, made his crafty whore the queen of Athens.

The first time onstage, I am terrified. The checker tiles slope, and the tables for the customers are low and far away. I climb up all shaky, praying not to fall. I am supposed to straddle one leg on the stage and the other on the tabletop so the men can ride the bill up to my thong, so I try to figure out how to do it.

The club is empty. Only one man is sitting at the table next to the stage. He is tall and his shirt is very clean. He nods hello, showing a set of the most beautiful teeth I have ever seen, and puts the folded bill on the edge of the stage. I take my shoe off to pick up my first dollar with my toes, like Heather can. He frowns at the dirty streaks on my skin. My legs were sweaty when I was dressing and the dust from the dressing-room floor got stuck. I rub the darkest spot against the other shin, but he stops me. I don't mind, he says, and scratches his fingernails up my leg. I relax a little. Maybe he'll be nice.

Show me your pussy, he says.

Weeknights are reserved for the regulars. The club owners insist on it being a friendly, family atmosphere. The girls sit around the stage in between sets and eat Chinese or Indian food. Dope circulates freely among the white girls and some of the customers, although girls with tracks on their arms are not allowed. The no-drug policy is strict for black girls. If a black girl has bad or dry skin, she is taken off the schedule. We call this stripping death.

After a month I am awarded an early weekend shift. Pete likes you, Jimmy says, and he thinks you'll do well. It's a big deal to get a shift on a Friday afternoon. A lot more money, but Peter spends time with his family, and Giannis, the weekend manager, is an asshole. The girls call him The Cunt. He enforces a no-bare-feet rule on the stage, not while drinking, not even in the bathroom. The toilet stalls have to stay open and every ten minutes he storms in, swings the front door open before we have a chance to answer, and waits until someone actually goes to the bathroom. One of the girls volunteers to pee in front of him. That satisfies him for half an hour, so we can get high in peace.

Giannis hates me. Hates that he has to take a girl like me, an Eastern European peasant, to work the stage at a high-class bar. You can pull that drug shit with the niggers, he threatens, but not here. If you don't get your shit together, you'll never work in the most lucrative of all bars, especially an early shift on Fridays, now that the place is filled with crazy Hasidim throwing money even at the ugly girls. So you better drag yourself out there and have a drink, and an expensive drink, no fucking five-dollar soda or a goddamn beer. Dream girls don't drink beer.

On Friday and Saturday nights the place is full of rappers or aspiring bullshit artists, as Mercedes, the prettiest of the light-skinned girls, calls them. She and I chase the dragon in secret, and give twenties to the other girls to watch so Giannis doesn't catch us.

Mercedes Diaz. Mercedes, the Beauty. Mercedes. Africa and China mingle evenly in her face. Her eyes glow like black pearls slightly filed at the corners. In her air, pure pride and dignity. She arrests everybody. Even the waitresses stop to see how she will open the set. She doesn't have to do anything wild. She can climb the steps, put her beaded purse down, and take her dress off lazily without even looking at the guys. The bills cascade.

Sometimes there are a few guys who are for real. Members of gangs, or real artists working on their albums. They sit in the back and stay cool. If we can get them going, then we have ourselves a party. One of them takes over the music. Pockets full of cash seal Giannis's mouth. The guys hop on the stage and dance with us, chant, Go sister, sister, and throw their rings and gold chains at us. One of them, a young boy, probably younger than me, wraps his chain with a ruby-eyed sphinx hanging off of it around my neck and says, Girl, red's your color.

A brother from the Big Easy told me that already, I say.

He laughs and says, Have a drink with me. Please.

14

I can't remember what street it was on, or
what day of the week it was, that I met Jay,
just the year and that it was Franco, one of
the dealers I knew from Gordon's, who
introduced us.

I drop my head down when I see them walking toward me,
hoping to cross the street before Franco recognizes me.

Hola, Sacha. He does anyway, and he mispronounces my
name like he always does when he hollers at me, when I'm
onstage.

Hola, Franco.

¿Tu me conoces? He grins. We never actually met, never
had a drink together.

Sí, I say. Everybody knows you.

The man next to him is serious. He is wearing the clean-
est, whitest T-shirt I've ever seen. He steps forward and says,
Hola, Sasha. Says it right. Says, Gorgeous hair, *Bonita*. He

kisses my hand. No one's ever kissed my hand before and now I understand what the fuss is all about.

Jay runs the most successful heroin operation in the East Village, called the Laundromat, on Seventh Street between Avenues B and C, and is a member of the Latin Kings. The line for his spot is so long that it sometimes coils all the way from the middle of the long block between Avenues B and C to Sixth Street. Hard-rock boys from the 7B Bar down shots of Jack Daniel's, shoot pool, and scoff at the loser junkies obediently standing in line.

He has a black belt in some martial art I can never remember, a two- or three-word slogan that ties him to Bruce Lee. He is vegan and never drinks. He also runs a small martial arts school for the kids in the neighborhood that he funds with his money. There are no requirements, other than that their parents have to be junkies, and the kids have to speak Spanish and stay clean.

Jay likes me the way KC liked me. I am not sure what that is, but the feeling is the same, and my thirst for dope is a little quieter. We are not lovers. We never became lovers. But I loved him. I love him still.

We walk together. We take long walks in Tompkins Square Park. He gives five-dollar bills to the homeless, who know him and call him Papa Jay. We feed pigeons with expensive Italian bread from Veniero's bakery. I beg him to go inside a bar with me. Any bar.

We don't have to be in the neighborhood, I plead. Please. Alcohol is the root of all evil, he says.

I thought money was, I say.

He stops and thinks about it. You're right, he says.

I tell him all my stories. About Mother. About KC. About the family. Even about Cousin, and how I got here. He listens. And understands, I think. I wish I was there for you then, he says, instead of those cocksuckers. But I'm here now, he promises. Here, take this, for protection, he says, and gives me a gun.

I have no idea why Jay gave me that gun. If he were alive, I'd ask him. I'd buy him a drink he could ignore and I'd ask him. I imagine seeing him on the street, passing him casually like college buddies do, screaming, Goddamn, it is you, how the hell are you, and they throw each other in the air and talk for a while.

Sometimes he tricks me, shows up wearing KC's face, or Scott's narrow body. For a moment I am fooled, but then I recognize that gun in his hand.

I am always happy to see him, and I always ask, Why did you give me that gun, man?

No matter whose face, whose body, he is wearing, he says the same thing.

To make you strong, *Bonita*, to make you strong.

. . .

Every morning I go over to Jay's school and practice ballet at the bar. He wants me to take a bath first and shave between my legs although he doesn't ask to see it. When I come out of the shower he gives me a brand-new pair of tights and a T-shirt. Then he sits in a corner and watches me dance.

Everybody in the area knows I spend time with Jay, and Jay never spends time with girls, so now I get free drinks, and people with me get free drinks, and the Chinese guy gives me extra dumplings, and Scott's friends tell him he is a lunatic and he should ask me to move out.

This guy can hurt you, man, hurt you bad, Howie warns.

They're just friends, Scott says.

Sure.

Jay doesn't care that I live with Scott, just as long as I take my afternoon baths and do my double turns. He gives me money for rent, food, clothes. Some days I am happy with all the money and I spend it on all my friends, or people I don't know. Then I see Scott's pretty white face get long with sadness, and I am ashamed, and I go and hug him, which means thank you, thank you for never asking me where the money comes from.

I am lying down on the mat at the school and Jay kisses me for the first time, on my breasts through the spandex. I want you to kick dope, he tells me and pulls away. That was the closest he ever got. It worries me you are getting so skinny. There are two boys sitting on the stoop outside and they snicker.

The guys in the neighborhood are not allowed to sell to you anymore, he says.

Are you kidding? I sit up, my back stiffening.

I never kid.

That was true. It was scary and I didn't want Jay to run my life.

They won't sell to any of your friends or your boyfriend.

I wince a little when he mentions Scott.

Listen, he says and squeezes my arm. I want you to kick dope and move away from here. Uptown, somewhere away from all this shit. I'll give you money.

Will you come? I ask.

I'll be fine around here. This is my turf.

I keep away for three days, and Jimmy puts me back on the schedule at Gordon's. Jay shows up within an hour. I can see Giannis knows who he is and is afraid of him. Jay waves me over as soon as he sits down. Let me finish the set, I wave back.

Sit here, he says.

I sit and say nothing.

I hate this, he says.

It's just money.

I'll give you money. He looks tense.

Are you all right? I touch his arm.

I'm fine. Just everyday shit. And I was worried about you.

We say nothing until the Turkish waitress, Ester, brings him a seltzer. Her hair hangs past her ass and she thinks it's beautiful. As she walks away he whispers, I bet she sometimes gets shit on it.

You're psycho, I laugh.

It's time for you to leave here, he tells me. Get clean. You won't be dancing here anymore.

I smoke a joint on my way to the apartment. I walk up the stairs inside the building. The little boy who lives with Ace is sitting on the last one.

Hey, I say.

Hey, he replies.

Scott and Ace are chasing the dragon. They have to smoke it, Scott says. Fucking waste. There were no syringes for sale on the street. I have no energy to face Ace's grin. Scott thinks Ace is his friend now. He stole our portable CD player and I don't have the heart to tell Scott. I feel like popping him one whenever he is over.

Have you heard any good CDs lately? I ask to get rid of his smile, and it works.

There's mail for you on the fridge, Scott tells me. It's from home.

It's a telegram. I am sure it's bad news and I don't want any bad news. I am high already and it's a smooth high, and who knows when the next one is coming, so I don't want anything to ruin it. I step outside to the hallway and sit on the stoop next to my little neighbor.

Hi, I say.

He ignores me this time.

Where's your dog?

On the terrace, he says. Ace don't let him in the house when johns come to visit Mom so he don't mess up the carpet while no one's looking.

Is Ace your dad?

No. He sits up. My dad is a soldier.

I love soldiers, I say.

Me too.

Are any of the johns around right now? I ask.

Uh-huh.

Do you want to go to the bodega and get some ice cream?

I'm not supposed to leave here.

Then I'll get you some. What kind do you like?

I don't know. Ace won't let Mom get me any. He says it's bad for the teeth and he don't want to spend a fortune on the teeth that are going to fall out soon anyway.

I'll pick you a good kind, fuck Ace, I say, and his little eyes spread with fear. Don't worry. I can say that. I'm badass.

As I go down the stairs, I stop and turn around.

What's your name?

Alfred.

I'm Sasha.

Alfred is not on his stoop when I come back, but his seat is still warm. I sit there and eat his vanilla and chocolate ice cream. The door to our apartment opens and Ace comes out, grinning again.

I love how you eat that ice cream, he says.

I say nothing, and go back inside the apartment, past Scott, past the dope on the table, and past the telegram on the refrigerator.

* * *

I hardly ever forget things. Words especially. Why, then, don't I remember the words from that telegram? I remember the searing in my chest, but not the words. I remember the envelope. It was white and wrinkled, stained from Scott's sweaty hand. I tore along its back. The postmark was from Livno, Mother's hometown. Aunt Dika would have walked for miles on foot to get to the post office. The paper inside the envelope was blue.

Juma killed herself. After her only friend, Caleb, moved away, she became obsessed with mirrors and one afternoon they found her next to a broken mirror with her throat slit. As always a miracle surrounded her. Her throat didn't bleed at all and there was very little blood on the glass. I remember the unevenness of Aunt Dika's writing. The ink blotches. Her hands probably shook. Maybe she was thinking of what to say next, or probably talking to the post office lady, and asking for more paper.

Maybe Juma missed me. Maybe she forgot that I too had moved and maybe she walked around the house like a ghost, haunting, looking for me behind the statues, paintings, and in her favorite mirror.

I remember that pain was sharp. And I remember not calling for years after that. What difference would it have made?

I sit around the apartment with the gun all night. I unzip the front of my pants and place it against the flesh of my lower belly until it is warm and no longer uncomfortable. Then I put it in my mouth. It tastes bitter and burns the sides of my tongue.

I stay up until dawn with the last bag of dope in my pocket calling me, and I drink and drink until I throw up. With nausea tearing at my guts, I flush the bag of dope to stop myself from snorting it. I immediately regret it, and try to catch it as it goes down, but it's lost. I think it's a sign, that I should get away from it for good, but then I get angry at myself because my trip is stupid. There are no such things as signs. And then I drink some more, and the room is no longer spinning, it's jumping, and so is my diaphragm, followed by a feeble trickle of yesterday's sweet and sour chicken.

Scott finds me passed out in the hallway with the gun in my pants. I am not sure how I got there, and he doesn't ask me anything for a while. He just plops down on the couch.

Everybody says you fuck him, he says.

Yeah? Well, I don't.

Should I try copping on Orchard Street? he asks.

I'm gonna lay off of it for a while.

Are you leaving me? he asks.

I don't know.

This fucking sucks!

He takes his jacket and leaves the apartment, and I have no urge to stop him.

I walk across the hall and knock as hard as I can on the door. I hope Ace is alone.

He opens the door.

Who're you with? I ask.

Solo. The girl's out.

What about Alfred?

Asleep downstairs.

Can I come in?

I knew you'd be here sooner or later, he says, and he closes the door.

. . .

I didn't lie to Scott when I said I didn't know if I was leaving. I just wasn't sure yet. I didn't know there would be no place to return to until Ace rolled off me and said, You'd be worth every penny, girl.

I put my clothes on, petted the little dog on the head, and went back to my apartment.

There were only a few hours left in that night, and I spent them alone, drinking. I remember maybe fifteen minutes. I tried twirling a pen on the table surface, and couldn't keep it from falling off the edge. It was a pen Scott brought home from work, and we were going to use it to write our checks, once we had a checking account. I remember wanting to throw up each time I hung my head down to pick it up off the floor.

I remember holding my hands in front of me and looking at them. Dope had melted my body down a few sizes and my fingers gained longer, sophisticated lines that reminded me of Mother. I was proud of that.

I don't know if Scott ever came home that night.

. . .

I eat a bagel and some yogurt the next day. Then I walk to the bodega to buy a paper with apartment ads. A French woman is looking for a roommate on Dyckman Street, all the way up-town around 200th Street. Far enough, I think, and hop on the subway.

200th Street in early October is filled with people like a watermelon with seeds. Spanish women and men fly by me. I ring a doorbell. It's almost dark and I am feeling the with-drawal, so I take a sip from my Jägermeister flask. The woman takes a long time to get to the door and when she finally does, at first she can't remember talking to me on the phone.

She has a hip problem, dysplasia, she explains, but surgery is against her spiritual belief so she meditates her pain away. The apartment has only one bedroom, which would be mine for $215 if I am interested.

I am.

She and her daughter will take the living room, share the sofa bed, until she figures out something else. I can have the bed. The woman, Bobbie, she calls herself, has lived most of her life in France, lost a husband in some sort of an accident, and she now speaks to her daughter in French so she doesn't forget where she is from. I can see the girl hates her already but is not old enough to know it.

What brings you all the way uptown? she asks.

Downtown, I say.

The East Village? she asks and it seems like she understands.

Uh-huh.

Where are you from?

Far.

It is hard, she says. Being far away.

Suddenly she looks nicer. Even the girl relaxes and looks at me. I'll manage all right with these people.

Outside, salsa blasts from every window. My future new neighbors have placed the speakers in the windows and, I think, are competing. That will be my new street. Those will be the sounds I listen to. The walk back to the subway is calm. I step on a crinkled newspaper with ads for cheap jackets and bedding on sale, pick it up, and put it in my pocket. It will be nice to own some sheets.

. . .

I stop at the Hut for a last drink. A tall guy I have never seen before is sitting on the other side of the bar with half a pint in front of him. Megan, the bartender, is cleaning the bar.

So, I try to be funny, when are you going to get some olives and cherries and peanuts to keep at the bar?

She looks at me, her pretty blue eyes foggy from dope, like an overcast afternoon, pours me tequila all the way up to the lip of a huge cocktail glass, brings it over instead of chasing it down the bar, and says, I'm sorry, we don't have anything like that.

I was kidding, I tell her and touch her arm. Sorry.

She looks even sadder, and as soon as I finish half of my shot she pours tequila from another bottle.

On the house too. She whispers, Just from a different bottle. Don't want the boss to catch on, she explains.

What do I have to do to get that kind of treatment around here? the tall guy asks.

Drop dead, she tells him, and I tip her plenty.

Jay is with a bunch of boys at his school. They are running around and playing. I decide not to go in. I stand behind the reflective glass and I watch him. He walks toward the window and looks past me. He can't see me. I knock right in front of his mouth.

Who is it, he asks, unphased.

Me.

He comes out. I stand in the same place until our eyes meet. He knows. I know. He nods his head and touches his heart with his right hand. I give him back the gun.

Good-bye, *Bonita*, he says. I am proud of you.

Take care of my Scott.

He won't let me, he says, and hands me a thick bundle of bills.

Take care of him anyway.

.   .   .

Scott is sleeping when I enter the apartment. His hair smells like sweet smoke, or a lightly grilled fig, warm and juicy. I want to touch him, whisper, I love you baby, I will always love you baby, but I'm afraid to wake him. What would I tell him— that I am a terrible coward running away?

He turns on his back and a little trickle of sleep-water seeps down his cheek. We bought the shirt he is wearing on the street together and I have washed it many times. I pack only my leather jacket, some of my clothes in the small bag, and my favorite CD. I never developed sophisticated taste in music. I just like pretty songs. Scott is pretty. I leave the Public Enemy CD on the stereo, next to two hundred dollars in a pile, hoping he'll use the money to pay the rent, and not miss me too much.

Alfred is on the stoop again.

The dog is sick, he tells me.

I go inside the door. Ace is high, his face sunk into his chest. I sneak by him quietly. There is a tumble in the bathroom. I open the door and the dog runs out between my feet.

I think of Grandmother and how she hated little dogs. Useless rats, she called the small litter we once had. Shoo, shoo, she chased after them as they tripped on their little bellies fat from worms, the chicken shit they munched on, and the wet bread we fed them.

I pick up the dirty little thing and run downstairs. Be quiet, be quiet, I tell him, we are out of here. Outside a Moishe's Moving Truck is stuck behind another car. I see the driver's tired-looking face, exhausted from carrying somebody else's possessions, somebody with enough to fill a truck. The warm bundle that is now mine is whimpering inside my sweater and I am glad I don't have to sleep alone.

My new bed is big, uneven, lonely. Moishe—I gave him his new name during the subway ride—is snoring by my feet. I bought him some milk and ham. Outside, people are fighting, screaming, *Maricón, Pendejo,* and I think of Cuba, of Lupe and Benya, and wonder what Roderigo is doing tonight, if Gordana ever married a rich man, if Dika still sips brandy for breakfast and calls it medicine. I wonder if the soccer is still as good as it was in the golden age, whether Father is sleeping or reading right now.

I hope that Alfred gets to go to school, that Heather gets clean, and that Sally likes the woman she will become. My stomach growls for dope. I offer it three huge sips of Jägermeister and a double dose of NyQuil and lie still as the warm comfort chases a wave of withdrawal to the surface of my skin. The dog moves up on the bed, closer to me, and I can hear him breathe calmly.

Don't worry, I whisper in his little ear.

Outside, the police siren wails like an alarm. I hope Scott will get to work on time. In all the rush I forgot to set the clock.

ABOUT THE AUTHOR

NATASHA RADOJČIĆ was born in Belgrade. In her
early twenties, on her own, she came to New York
City, earned an MFA from Columbia University,
and stayed. She is the author of *Homecoming*.

ABOUT THE TYPE

The text of this book was set in Filosofia. It was
designed in 1996 by Zuzana Licko, who created it
for digital typesetting as an interpretation of the
sixteenth-century typeface Bodoni. She has
designed many typefaces and is the cofounder
of *Emigre* magazine, where many of them first
appeared. Filosofia, an example of Licko's unusual
font designs, has classical proportions with a
strong feeling, softened by rounded droplike serifs.

RADOJCI   Radojcic, Natasha.

        You don't have to
        live here.

$21.95

DATE			